"You should la[...] becomes you."

"Oh, really?" Hank [...] his hand and turned her face back to him. "How so?"

In the light from the bunkhouse he could see her eyes clearly now. They were blue, he noticed for the first time. And not for the first time, he could see how beautiful she was.

"When you smile or laugh, your face lights up," Andrea said softly, tentatively. "You're handsome when you do."

"Am I handsome now?" he asked, giving her a hint of a smile.

She averted her eyes.

"I'll take that as a yes."

More than anything he wanted to kiss this woman, to take her in his arms and surrender to the tension he felt around her since the first day he met her. But something was holding him back.

He couldn't quite put his finger on it.

"Can I ask you something, Hank?"

"Of course," he replied.

"Why do you seem so dead set against marriage?"

Dear Reader,

There's only one bachelor left on the Lazy L Ranch these days. So, of course, this is his book. Hank Ledbetter's sister and brother have already met their matches and have taken the walk down the aisle, but he's not buying into the idea of happily-ever-after. In fact, he's vowed to remain a bachelor for the rest of his days.

When his brother-in-law signs him up to give horseback riding lessons to a rich young woman, he's downright angry. When Hank meets Andrea Jacobs at the airport, he's not impressed with her elegant hairdo or her expensive clothes. And she has the nerve to not be that interested in talking to him on the drive to the ranch. He had intended to ignore her, but she's beat him to it!

During a lesson, Hank and Andrea are forced into doing some tough riding, and Hank is impressed with her stamina. Ultimately, he finds himself drawn to her.

Only after she has him truly hooked does Andrea pull back. He's becoming too possessive and she has made a promise to herself she must fulfill. But can she still have a chance with Hank, or is it too late? Help comes in the form of some women on the Lazy L who are all hoping, praying and working for Hank and Andrea's happy ending.

Enjoy!

Judy Christenberry

Judy Christenberry
THE CHRISTMAS COWBOY

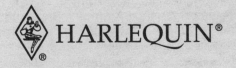

HARLEQUIN®

TORONTO • NEW YORK • LONDON
AMSTERDAM • PARIS • SYDNEY • HAMBURG
STOCKHOLM • ATHENS • TOKYO • MILAN • MADRID
PRAGUE • WARSAW • BUDAPEST • AUCKLAND

ISBN-13: 978-0-373-75238-6
ISBN-10:   0-373-75238-5

THE CHRISTMAS COWBOY

Printed in U.S.A.

ABOUT THE AUTHOR

Judy Christenberry has been writing romances for more than nineteen years because she loves happy endings as much as her readers do. A former French teacher, Judy now devotes herself to writing full-time. She hopes readers have as much fun with her stories as she does. She spends her spare time reading, watching her favorite sports teams and keeping track of her two daughters. Judy lives in Texas. You can find out more about Judy and her books at www.judychristenberry.com.

Books by Judy Christenberry

HARLEQUIN AMERICAN ROMANCE

*Brides for Brothers
**Children of Texas
‡Dallas Duets
†The Lazy L Ranch

Chapter One

Hank Ledbetter was hungry.

After a long day in the saddle he couldn't wait to devour the meal his sister had waiting in the kitchen at the Lazy L. But Jessica allowed no one to eat until the entire family was at the table. Whatever was left of the family, he thought.

Right now his brother, Pete, was on his honeymoon, as was his grandfather Cliff and his new bride, Leslie. Jess, too, had married only last summer.

Yes, the Ledbetters were dropping like flies.

Hank's belly growled. There'd be no wedding in *his* future.

All he was concerned with was eating his dinner and getting to town to see the ladies. He wasn't picky about his women. Brunettes, blondes, redheads… Didn't matter to Hank, as long as they made him laugh and weren't empty between the ears.

And weren't interested in roping themselves a cowboy for a husband.

"Jess, can't we at least get started without Jim?" After a full day's work, Hank needed nourishment.

His sister shook her head. "Hold your horses. He had to take a phone call. I'm sure he'll be here in a minute."

"Can't he just tell them we're closed until December?"

"No, he can't, Hank. You know that."

He should've known Jess would think Jim did the right thing, no matter what. After all, hadn't Jim agreed last summer to wait for a honeymoon until October—it was now November—when the Lazy L dude-and-cattle ranch was closed to guests until December? Not many men would be willing to postpone what Hank assumed was the best part of marriage.

Not that he would ever find out, he told himself again as he shook his head. He was having too much fun. He and Jim had split their jobs so that neither had to work every day, which left Hank plenty of time for the social life he was enjoying in nearby Steamboat Springs.

At the sound of boot heels, he looked up. "'Bout time you got here. I'm starving."

Jim Bradford kissed his wife before he took a seat. "That's why it pays to be married to the cook," he said with a grin.

Jessica joined them at the table and Jim said the blessing. As she started passing the dishes, she asked, "Who was it on the phone?"

"It was an interesting call," Jim said as he took a bite of a freshly baked roll. He looked up at Hank. "Means you won't have to take care of the cattle anymore, Hank. You're in charge of the horses."

On one hand, that was good news, since Hank preferred horses to cows anytime. But he didn't understand why the change.

"What are you talking about, Jim?"

"That call was from a young woman who needs to learn to ride in a month. She's willing to pay a lot for lessons."

Jess asked the question that was on Hank's mind. "Why's she coming here?"

"She says she heard about us from a friend of a friend."

This time Hank spoke first. "Where's she from?"

"New York City."

Hank's hand stilled on its way to his mouth, the beef stew dripping from his fork. "A city woman is coming all the way to Colorado to learn to ride? Can't she learn in New York?"

"She wants to learn to ride like a cowboy." Jim dug in to his food. "Anyway, she's going to take the bedroom next to ours, with the private bath."

"This isn't fair! I was supposed to have the whole month off. No guests till December—that was the deal."

"Except for tending the horses, that's true," Jim said calmly. "And that's why you'll receive extra pay for the month. Can't you use a little extra cash?"

"I think I'd rather tend the horses half the week and tend the ladies the other half." Hank couldn't help the smile that lit his dark eyes.

Jim named a figure. "You sure you can't use the money? I did promise the woman, after all."

The amount was tempting. Still... "Why don't *you* teach her to ride!" He had to hold his ground, or Jim and Jess would trot all over him the way they did last summer when the family decided to turn the cattle ranch into a dude ranch. Hank was the only holdout. He'd given Jess so much resistance that his granddad had called in an outside manager. Once Jim came, he not only stole his sister's heart, he whipped Hank into shape. But Jim wasn't getting his way this time.

"Then you'd have to deal with the ranch by yourself," Jim replied calmly. "And you wouldn't get the extra money. And you'd have to work six days a week."

Jim had a point. After all, he couldn't expect Jess to fill in for Mary Jo, Pete's wife and the ranch chef, and work the herd at the same time.

"Damn it, Jim, I didn't volunteer for this job."

"I know, Hank. But one of us has to teach her. And my wife isn't much in favor of me giving private lessons to a single lady." He winked at Jess. "But it's your choice, Hank. Either teach the lady to ride for a month or tend the horses and work the herd six days a week."

Hank ground his teeth. He didn't like either choice.

"Did she say she was staying until she learned to ride, or the full month?"

"She's paying in advance for a full month, so she's staying."

"Damn, damn, damn," Hank muttered.

"It won't be that bad, Hank," Jess interjected. "She'll probably be too sore to ride much in the beginning."

"True, Jess," her husband concurred. He turned to Hank. "And you've got to promise not to try to get rid of her before the end of the month. Be nice to her."

Hank frowned at Jim again. "Fine," he said.

He picked up his fork again, but the food that had enticed him only minutes ago no longer appealed. He pushed away from the table.

"With my luck she'll be three hundred pounds and ugly as sin."

HANK FOUND HIMSELF in the Denver airport two days later. He'd made an effort to clean himself up, wearing a nice western shirt with pressed jeans, a belt buckle he'd won in a Cheyenne rodeo and his dress Resistol hat. He was even wearing his dress boots, all for this wealthy woman.

Jess had given him the seal of approval before he left the ranch earlier that morning. Then she'd handed him a sign to hold up, with the lady's name printed on it. Andrea Jacobs.

Her name made her sound stuck up. Just one more fault to add to the long list Hank had drawn up in his mind. His imagination had already turned her into one damn near impossible woman.

He leaned against the wall in the baggage-claim area, watching people come and go. When the first group of travelers came through the door, he held up the sign, figuring she'd be traveling first-class. A rather large woman came through the door, and Hank grimaced behind the placard, certain she had to be the one.

"Excuse me," said a voice beside him. "I'm Andrea Jacobs."

He turned his head and stared. Slender and young, the woman had long, wavy, brown hair that shone with red highlights. She was more than pretty. "You are?" he asked, shocked by her appearance—and his luck.

"Last time I checked my ID I was." The woman smiled and showed perfect white teeth. "Thank you for holding up a sign. Your manager said to look for a tall man with a cowboy hat, but—" she looked around "—there seem to be a lot of tall men with cowboy hats in the terminal."

He stiffened a bit. "It's ranch country, ma'am." He wanted to remind her she wasn't in New York anymore, but held his tongue. "Did you bring luggage?"

She looked at him as if he was crazy. "You expected me to arrive without luggage for a month's stay?"

Little Miss Andrea Jacobs sure had an attitude. He was beginning to wish the heavyset woman he'd spotted earlier was his new pupil. She might have been easier to manage. "Let's get your bags, then," he growled.

It wasn't what he wanted to say, but he'd promised his sister and brother-in-law he'd be on best behavior.

ANDREA JACOBS was irritated.

She followed the cowboy to the baggage-claim area and now he just stood there as the luggage spun around on the carousel. He hadn't asked her what her bags looked like. Were they going to wait until everyone else had claimed their luggage?

What kind of man was this?

He hadn't even bothered to introduce himself when they met.

When she'd decided to take these lessons, she'd had

all these romantic notions about a cowboy who would teach her how to ride. Maybe she'd read too many books and seen too many westerns, but she'd expected a strong, old-fashioned kind of man, one who could ride like the wind and rope a rustling steer, but treat a woman like a prized possession.

Instead she got *him*.

When the couple beside her heaved their bags off the carousel, he finally turned to her. "How many bags do you have?"

"Three. They're bright blue," she said begrudgingly.

She began to think that maybe this hadn't been the best idea. Maybe she should never have decided to learn to ride just so she could impress her—

"Aren't you even looking for your luggage?"

She turned to him. "Excuse me?"

"You look like you're daydreaming and meanwhile a couple of blue bags have been going around. I don't know what your suitcases look like, so you'd best pay attention."

This oaf wasn't anything like the nice man from the Lazy L dude ranch she'd spoken to on the phone. He'd promised she'd be a great rider in a month and gather memories to last a lifetime.

"Are those your bags coming up?" His impatient voice intruded on her thoughts again.

She looked up. "Yes, those three."

She grabbed two of the bags and set them at her feet. Then he chased after the third bag.

"I'll carry the middle bag," she said when he returned.

"I can manage," he said tersely.

"Fine." She'd been trying to be gracious but if he insisted on carrying everything, then so be it. She stepped back so he could lead the way to his vehicle. She only hoped it was comfortable. She'd gotten up very early this morning to catch her flight. Though she'd planned to sleep on the flight, she'd sat next to a woman who had talked to her the entire trip.

Certainly, Mr. Sourpuss wouldn't intrude on her naptime.

Though she'd have liked to stop somewhere for lunch, she wouldn't suggest such a nicety to this man. The sooner they got to the ranch, the better.

His vehicle was a late-model Lexus sedan. She could take a nice nap in that car. He stowed her luggage in the trunk, then opened the passenger-side door for her. The small courtesy warmed her, but she certainly wasn't won over yet.

When he pulled the car into traffic, she expected he'd talk about the ranch, but he was quiet, only the sounds of country music on the radio preventing total silence.

Fine with her. She lay her head back and was almost asleep when she felt the car slowing. "Is something wrong?"

"I'm hungry," the cowboy replied.

Looking around, she noticed they'd pulled into the parking lot of a restaurant called The Prime Rib. She inhaled the scent of barbecued beef.

"The ranch is two hours away. I need to eat." With that he got out of the car.

Andrea sat there, not sure if she should follow.

Her door opened. "Are you getting out?"

"I'm sorry. I didn't understand that you…" Never mind, she told herself. She simply got out of the car and followed him into the restaurant.

The place was much nicer than she would expect the oaf beside her to frequent.

When they were seated and the server approached their table, he barked, "We'll take a 'mucho nacho' and two iced teas to start."

"Are the nachos good?" Andrea asked when the waitress left, trying to make conversation, though she didn't know why she was bothering.

"I like them."

She tried again. "I'm surprised you ordered an iced tea. I figured you for a beer man."

He shot her a look. In the bright light she could see that his eyes were dark brown laced with topaz. Almost the same brown as his hair, now that he'd taken off his hat.

"Jess said I couldn't."

"Is he your boss?"

"No. *She's* my sister."

She nodded. "So you both work on the ranch?"

"No, we both *own* the ranch," he said indignantly. Then he added, "Along with my grandfather and my brother."

"And you are…?"

"Hank Ledbetter." He flushed. She could tell he'd suddenly realized he'd forgotten to introduce himself.

The waitress arrived then with a towering plate of nachos and their drinks. Before Andrea could order for herself, Hank ordered for both of them. "Two sirloins, medium rare, with baked potato and salad."

True, Andrea thought, she was more than two thousand miles from home, but she'd never expected to find a totally different species of man in Colorado. She sat there, completely dumbfounded at his audacity.

"Aren't you going to try the nachos?" he asked when he noticed her sitting there stiffly.

Much as she didn't want to, she was hungry. "Are they hot?"

"Not if you don't eat those green things. They're jalapeños. That's what makes them hot."

She laughed to herself. "We do have jalapeños in New York, Mr. Ledbetter. In fact, we have all kinds of cuisine."

She tried some of the nachos and found them delicious.

They ate in silence, Hank wolfing down three times as much as she did. When only one chip remained, he said, "You want that?"

"No, thanks. You go ahead."

He didn't hesitate. Scooping up the chip, he ate it in one bite.

She marveled at his appetite. "Will you be able to eat your steak?" she asked.

His brow knit as he looked at her. "Why wouldn't I?"

"I just thought that after you... Never mind. I guess that was a dumb question."

Their meals arrived then and she sighed when she saw the huge, thick steak.

"I'll never be able to eat all that," she said, giving voice to her thoughts. "That's more than I eat in two dinners back in New York."

The cowboy's eyes raked over her face and neck, breasts and waist. "You could use some meat on your bones."

"Excuse me?" she sputtered.

"Trust me. Once you're in the saddle all day, you'll eat everything that's put in front of you."

The man wasn't only rude, Andrea thought. He was downright crazy.

HANK COULDN'T BELIEVE the woman was sleeping while they were driving through the most beautiful countryside in the world. They were coming down the mountain, the picturesque town of Steamboat Springs lying just below them.

She'd fallen asleep about half an hour after leaving Denver. He wouldn't have known if he hadn't snuck a look at her. It was obvious he hadn't needed to worry about her chattering nonstop.

At lunch, what little talking they'd done had made him think they spoke different languages. Sometimes she made sense, but other times he had no idea what she was talking about.

But he'd made a promise to be polite. And he'd tried. It was certainly easier now that she was asleep.

Taking liberties, he snatched glances at her as he drove. Her wavy hair curved around high cheekbones, and rosy lips were set in a pout. His eyes roamed lower, to her full breasts and slender waist, exposed now that she'd removed her coat in the warm car. Her manicured hands rested on her lap. And her legs…long and shapely, just the way he liked 'em.

No, he told himself. *Do not go there.*

Andrea Jacobs might be beautiful, with curves in all the right places, but she was not the woman for him. Besides, he had lots of women in Steamboat Springs, ones he could understand. He didn't need a city slicker with an attitude—no matter how gorgeous she was.

"Where are we?"

The voice startled him and he wrenched his attention from her legs back to the road.

"Steamboat Springs," he said in a husky voice. He cleared his throat, pretending boredom. "The ranch is about fifteen minutes outside of town."

"I'm sorry. I didn't think I'd sleep that long."

"Not a problem." He didn't tell her that her nap had given him a chance to check out her lovely body.

She sat up and looked out the window. "This seems like a nice town. Not as big as I thought it would be, though."

"It has everything we need." His voice sounded perturbed, even to his own ears.

"I didn't mean anything by that," she was quick to explain. "It's just that…well, in comparison to New York, everything looks small."

"Really?" Hank said sarcastically.

"Mr. Ledbetter, I did not mean to insult your town."

"So you'd rather insult me?"

She crossed her arms, which only brought his attention back to her ample bosom.

He looked the other way before she caught him. He didn't think she'd appreciate his interest.

THE LAZY L LOOMED ahead of her, looking like a picture postcard. Nestled against the Rocky Mountains, the two-story ranch house, barn and numerous outbuildings wrapped in a split-rail fence were just what Andrea had expected.

Hank pulled the Lexus up to the main entrance. Before he could come around and open her door, she was out of the car, eager to meet her other hosts.

"This is beautiful," she said, looking around her.

"Yeah," Hank agreed, and she realized that was the first statement from her he didn't argue with.

He moved to the trunk to get her bags at the same time as the front door opened and a couple came out, followed by two Labrador puppies.

The young woman approached, her hand outstretched in greeting. "I'm Jessica Bradford. Welcome to the Lazy L."

"And I'm Jim Bradford. I spoke to you on the phone."

Andrea shook their hands. "You certainly have a lovely place."

"Thank you," Jessica said. "We'll leave your bags for the men to bring in. Let's get inside where it's warm." She whistled to the dogs, who followed obediently.

The house was everything Andrea thought it would be. Warm and rustic with western accents.

"Let's go into the living room. Jim built a fire and I made some treats for us."

"That's so nice of you. But your brother stopped at a restaurant on the way. I'm afraid I couldn't eat another bite."

"Hank will, though," Jessica said in a mock whisper. "In case you didn't notice, he's a bottomless pit."

Andrea laughed, and realized she felt comfortable for the first time since getting off the plane.

Everything was going to be fine, she told herself. She needn't worry. Jessica was friendly and the ranch was beautiful. The Lazy L was going to be the perfect place to learn to ride and put her plan into action.

Now all she had to do was steer clear of Mr. Sourpuss.

Andrea sat down on one of the sofas. "I'm eager to get started with my lessons," she began. "Can you introduce me to the cowboy who'll be my teacher?"

Jessica shot her a puzzled look. "Didn't Hank tell you? *He's* your teacher."

Chapter Two

Andrea felt her spirit fall like a boulder through water. She nearly sputtered when she tried to speak. "Wha… I…" She gave up.

"Is something wrong, Andrea?" her gracious hostess asked.

Wrong? Other than the fact that she was about to spend the next month with that grizzly bear of a man, what could be wrong?

Jessica's face fell. "Oh, no!" she cried. "What did he do?"

Andrea forced her mind to focus. Though she made a mental list of every one of Hank's offenses, she said nothing because Jim and the man himself walked in.

"So," Jim Bradford said. "Did you enjoy the trip from the airport?"

Before Andrea could reply, Hank spoke up. "She slept the whole way. Missed all that pretty scenery."

Jessica nearly gasped. "But surely you could understand, Hank. Miss Jacobs must have been up at the crack of dawn for her flight." Her eyes flashed at her brother.

Hank shrugged. "She didn't tell me that." He didn't hide his annoyance.

Andrea caught the look he shot her from under partly closed lids, and she wanted to scream. Surely there was another riding instructor at the ranch. There was no way she could spend a month with this irritating, stubborn boor.

Jim stepped forward and defused the situation. He smiled as he sat next to his wife. "So, Andrea, we're happy to have you. Have you ever been on a horse before?"

"No, I haven't."

Hank let out an audible groan.

She ignored him. "But I can be taught, right?"

Jim nodded. "Hank's a great teacher for an untrained rider."

"What brings you all the way to Colorado for riding lessons?" Hank asked from the doorway. He'd refused to sit. "No stables in New York?"

"As I told your brother-in-law on the phone I want to ride like a cowboy."

"We'll see. After all, I only have a month."

"I'm a quick study, Mr. Ledbetter."

He gave her a level look. "Again, we'll see." Then his gaze locked with hers. "Are there a lot of cowboys in New York City for you to ride with?"

"No. I...I'm going to visit someone after I leave here." Surely there was no harm in revealing that much, Andrea thought.

"Who?" Hank barked.

Andrea lowered her gaze. "No one you know, I'm sure."

"I don't think an inquisition is necessary, Hank," Jim interjected. "We're all glad Andrea chose us."

"Fine!" Hank snapped. "I'm going out to the barn to do what cowboys do." He stalked out of the room, calling for the dogs to follow.

Jim stood up. "I'd better go talk with your instructor." He nodded to his wife as he left.

When both men were out of earshot, Jessica turned to Andrea. "Was that how he behaved with you earlier?"

Andrea was reluctant to tell her. "Well, mostly. But I guess I'm to blame, too. I seem to say the wrong thing around him."

"Don't be sorry. My brother can be…uncivilized at times. But you won't find a better teacher east or west of the Rockies."

"I'm sure," Andrea said with a weak smile.

All she was really sure of was how long and painful the next month would be.

HANK DREADED the coming weeks. Thirty days of hell with an irritating city girl.

He'd managed to escape the homey little scene in the living room and was now in the horse barn mucking out stalls, venting his frustration by jamming the pitchfork into fresh hay.

He heard footfalls behind him and knew it was Jim. Coming to chew him out, no doubt.

"I thought for sure once you saw her you'd be dying to teach her," Jim said as he approached.

Hank didn't look up. "I'm not."

"Come on, Hank. She's quite a looker."

"Forget our deal. You give her lessons, then."

"You know Jess won't agree to that. Especially now that she's seen her."

Hank's eyes shot up. "You're attracted to her?" he asked, outrage in his voice.

Jim held up his hands. "Compared to Jess? Not on your life. Besides, I won't let you out of this. You agreed to take her on, and that's what's going to happen. Get used to it. We've got a business to run here."

Jim had a point, but Hank wouldn't concede it. Nor would he admit that ever since Jim had arrived at the Lazy L, his sister's idea of turning the family homestead into a dude ranch had worked better than he'd expected.

Instead, he said, "I think we ought to refuse her. Just send her on her way."

"I've got a better idea. You give her what she paid for."

Hank threw down the pitchfork.

"Fine. I'll teach her. But she's mine only for the lessons. The rest of the time you and Jessie entertain her."

"So, DID HE AGREE to be nice?" Jessica looked up from the casserole she was preparing when she heard her husband come in.

"Not exactly," Jim replied. He told her about the compromise of them having to entertain their guest.

Jessica shook her head. "I don't mind entertaining her when I can, but I don't understand him. We have a beautiful single woman here at the ranch and he has to go find other women? What's wrong with him?"

"He doesn't want to feel trapped. I understand him."

Jessica's brows rose. "Oh, really? You feel trapped with me?"

Jim reached out and pulled his wife into a bear hug. "You know what I mean." He gave her a kiss. "Give him time. He may change his mind."

"I doubt it. He's too wrapped up in the action in town. Those women are only out to capture him. They know that whichever one he chooses will be well provided for."

"I'm sure he'll realize that before it's too late."

"I hope so. It would make life miserable if he married a woman who wanted breakfast in bed every day."

Jim kissed his wife. "It'll work out. Don't worry. In the meantime—"

"Am I interrupting?"

They both turned to see Andrea at the door.

"I wasn't sure whether I was allowed in the kitchen."

Jessica ushered her in. "If we were in full guest mode, you wouldn't, simply because it gets too crowded in here with the staff. But since you're the only guest, we'll be using the kitchen to eat in. We have dinner at six."

Andrea smiled. "Good. I had visions of eating in the dining room all by myself. That would be horrible."

"Is everything all right in your room?"

"Yes, of course. It's lovely. And I was wondering if I'll be able to use a washer and dryer while I'm here."

"You can, but I'd be glad to do your laundry."

"I can do it. And you don't have to clean my room more than once a week."

"You're certainly making it easy for me," Jessica said. Then, as if remembering something, she gave a startled "Oh" then moved across the room to a counter where she picked up a box. "I forgot to put this in your room."

"What is it?" Andrea asked.

"Epsom salts. They'll help reduce the soreness you'll feel when you start riding. You fill your tub with hot water and pour in a cup of this before you soak."

Andrea cringed. "Will I be that sore?"

Jim laughed. "Horseback riding requires the use of some muscles that aren't used often."

"Then thanks, I think. I'll run this up to my room." She started, then stopped. "I was wondering, is there a store nearby where I can pick up some jeans for riding? I only have designer jeans and somehow I don't think they're the right thing to wear."

"There's a good place in town," Jessica said. "I suspect there're other things you'll need, too. We can go after dinner, if you want."

"Only if you let me come," Jim told his wife, wrapping his arms around her again and pulling her close.

Jessica grinned at him, then turned to Andrea. She smiled and wiggled her brows. "We're newlyweds, you know what I mean?"

Andrea returned the smile, but truthfully she didn't have a clue what she meant.

AT SIX O'CLOCK exactly Hank entered the kitchen. He'd managed to find chores to occupy his afternoon and had avoided his new guest. Now, freshly showered and dressed, he was hungry.

He sat down at the table in his usual spot and noticed the fourth place setting. "Who's joining us?" he asked his sister, though he was afraid to hear the answer.

Before Jess could reply, a small voice said, "I am."

He turned to find Andrea walking through the kitchen door.

"Is that a problem?" she asked when she took the seat across from him.

He shrugged. "Suit yourself. But guests usually eat in the dining room."

"Andrea's not a conventional guest, Hank," Jessie said as she put a platter of corn on the table, followed by a bowl of salad, biscuits and a steaming casserole. "She doesn't want a fuss. And I, for one, appreciate it."

Great, Hank thought. Just what he needed. Another "member of the family." The New York side, he joked to himself.

When Jim came in and Jess said the blessing, everyone served themselves.

"Where were you all afternoon?" Jess asked Hank as she filled her plate. "I was showing Andrea around the ranch and I thought we'd run into you."

"I had some things to do to get ready for tomorrow."

"Oh. Have you chosen a horse for Andrea?"

"Yeah."

Andrea spoke up. "Are you going to tell me about him?"

"Her," he corrected tersely. "It's a young mare I

bought last summer with an Appaloosa bloodline." Not that she'd know what that meant.

Jess asked, "Is that the one you bought from Dan Peters? She's—"

As she swallowed a forkful of salad, Andrea suddenly began to choke, coughing into her hand.

"Are you all right?" Hank asked, rising to his feet. "I could do the Heimlich on you, if you need."

"No!" Andrea managed to get out between coughs. "I'm fine." She cleared her throat and took a drink. "You were saying, Jessica?"

"I think she's a good choice, that mare. I rode her once or twice last summer. She's very gentle."

Hank nodded. "I think she'll be good for Miss Jacobs."

"Please, Hank, call me Andrea."

He looked at her in surprise. "Don't you think that's a little too informal for a New York socialite?"

Jim fairly groaned, but Andrea seemed unaffected. She calmly said, "It may surprise you to know that though my family is well-off, I do work. And I can actually cook and clean for myself."

"Really?" Hank tried for nonchalance, but he was actually intrigued. He thought she was a rich girl taken care of by daddy's millions. "What do you do?" he asked in spite of himself.

"I'm a graphic designer for a small advertising firm."

Hank could imagine that. Along with her real femininity and poise, she had an artsy quality about her, and wasn't that a perfect education for a rich girl? Art school. He could see her now, going to class dressed in her designer clothes and carrying her sketches in a designer bag. No doubt she took a cab to school or had the chauffeur drop her off. No public transit for this girl.

"And you managed to get a month off from work?" he asked skeptically.

He could swear Andrea hesitated just a second before she replied, "I had some vacation time saved up."

"Nice company." He took a forkful of chicken casserole and thought aloud as he chewed. "I can't even remember the last time I had a vacation."

"Think of this next month as one," Jim interjected. "You don't have to deal with the herd." He shot Hank a grin, and Jess laughed.

True, but he had to deal with Miss Jacobs. He wasn't sure which was worse.

After Andrea took her first bite of the casserole, she looked at Jessica. "This is delicious."

Jess smiled. "Thanks. I went to college for home ec." She laughed.

"Actually, public relations," Jim said.

"Sounds like the perfect preparation for your job."

"Oh, I don't usually cook. Hank's and my older brother, Pete, married our chef. Mary Jo does a wonderful job of cooking. They're on their honeymoon."

"Yeah, she does," Hank said. He looked at his sister, "You're not so bad yourself, sis."

"Thanks, Hank."

When Hank had finished his dinner, he stood up to leave.

"You don't want dessert?" Jess asked.

"You made dessert? Well, I might have some now that I think about it."

She brought a cake plate from the counter and lifted the lid, revealing a chocolate cake.

"Oh, my, and I was thinking about refusing dessert, but like Hank, I've changed my mind." Andrea smiled at Jessica.

"Good. I hope you like it, because you'll probably get it again tomorrow."

"I'm a chocoholic. You can't give me too much chocolate. Are you a chocoholic, Hank?"

"No, Miss Jacobs, I'm not. I have no addictions."

Andrea shot him a look, but Hank dove into his cake. He wolfed it down, then pushed away from the table. "If y'all will excuse me, I'm going to town."

Andrea looked up. "So are we."

Hank was startled. "Why?" he demanded.

"I need to do some shopping."

"You brought three bags! Isn't that enough clothes for you?"

"Apparently not," she said with a smile, refusing to be offended.

"Women!" Hank said as he stomped out of the kitchen. "I wouldn't be caught dead shopping."

"I THINK THIS STORE will have exactly what you need," Jessica said as they entered a large western clothing outlet in Steamboat Springs.

Andrea was surprised by how busy the town was for a weeknight. Every store was crowded. Some people looked to be tourists like her. In their fur jackets and Ugg boots they stood out from the regulars.

"Let's start with jeans," Jessica proposed as she led Andrea to the appropriate section.

Andrea followed, along with Jim. She'd helped the couple clean up the dishes and the kitchen after dinner in return for their help with her shopping.

Jessica picked out a few different styles and Andrea went into the dressing room to try them on.

When she emerged in one pair, Jessica and Jim nodded. "Perfect, Andrea," Jessica said. "How do they feel?"

"Like sausage casing," she said as she turned to view herself in the mirror. "And I'm the sausage."

Jess laughed. "Then they fit just right."

With Jessica's help, she bought three pairs of jeans and a handful of western-style shirts, a ski jacket, long underwear and a pair of gloves. And boots.

"You need one more thing—a cowboy hat," Jess said.

Andrea looked at her. "Are you sure?"

"Absolutely. But a hat's a tricky fit. It has to be tight enough so it won't fly off while you're riding, but not so tight it'll give you a headache. Jim will be more help there."

"She's right," Jim said with a grin. "I'm the hat man."

"I really appreciate it, Jim," Andrea said. "You're better at shopping than any man I know."

"Maybe you don't know many married men." Jim laughed.

"I guess I don't."

When Jim took her to the hat section, she was surprised to see so many choices. She'd always thought one cowboy hat looked like another.

Jim gave her several to try, none of which apparently was right, then he led her around the aisle to another rack.

She heard a woman's flirty laugh, followed by the rumble of a deep, sexy male voice. A voice she recognized.

Could it be?

She lifted her head so she could see from under the brim of the gray suede hat she'd tried on, and her eyes met a pair of brown ones shot through with topaz.

"Hank. What are you doing here? I thought you wouldn't be caught dead shopping."

He let go of the woman he'd been embracing and put a hat on her long blond tresses. "I'm helping a friend pick out a hat."

"I see," Andrea said. "Maybe you can give your opinion about *this* hat." She indicated the one she wore.

"A good choice," Hank grudgingly said. "Of course, it's also the most expensive."

The blonde he was with tried on a few more hats. Then she stepped close to him, slid her hands up Hank's chest and around his neck. "Ooh! I love this hat, Hank. Can I have it?"

He pulled her arms down. "Come on, Lucy, it's not appropriate for you."

"You just don't want to pay for it because it's so expensive."

"No, that's not the reason."

"Pretty please, Hank? The color looks good on me."

Andrea had to stifle a laugh as she noticed the lavender hat with an ostrich feather in red and purple encircling the crown.

"Fine, I'll get it for you."

She couldn't help herself. "Nice choice!" she called out.

The blonde smiled. "Thanks." Then she whispered something to Hank. Despite Hank's sharp no, she spoke up, anyway. "We're heading out for a drink and some dancing. Want to join us?"

Andrea shook her head. "Thanks, anyway. I've got an early day tomorrow." She wanted to remind Hank that he did, too, but she held her tongue.

It didn't matter to her what Hank Ledbetter did with his nights.

She watched him walk away with the blonde draped around him. If she didn't know better, she'd think that pang in her stomach was jealousy.

Chapter Three

Andrea came down to the kitchen early the next morning. She hadn't been able to sleep much in anticipation of her first riding lesson with Hank. She'd found Jessica already preparing breakfast, and lent a hand as they chatted.

They were laughing about some of the antics of previous guests when Hank entered the room and went directly to the coffeepot.

"You'd better eat a big breakfast or you'll be starving by lunch!" he snapped.

Andrea had thought they'd prepared too much food, but she must've been inspired by the early hour, for she cleaned her plate. Hank did the same.

When Hank got up from the table, Andrea jumped up, too. She wasn't going to be accused of dawdling.

Hank stared at her. "You ready?"

"Yes," she said, putting on her new ski jacket and hat, and working on her gloves as she followed Hank.

As they walked to the horse barn, Andrea felt anticipation grow. Along with fear. She hoped she managed to do what her teacher asked without showing she was scared.

"Okay, first you need to know the equipment you'll be using." Hank began pointing out the parts that they used to saddle a horse. After he made her repeat the names of the parts, he introduced her to the horse she was going to ride. "This is Moonbeam."

"Nice name."

"She came with it. Dan Peters named her."

Andrea stroked the horse several times under Hank's supervision.

Then he brought out an apple and cut it in half. "Here, hold this flat in your hand and feed it to her."

Andrea did as he said, refusing to ask if the horse would bite her. When the horse gently took the apple half and crunched it, Andrea stood amazed. Then she fed the mare the other half. When the animal nuzzled Andrea for more, Andrea looked at Hank. "Do you have more?"

"No. That's enough. We don't want to spoil her."

Andrea stroked Moonbeam's neck. But she watched Hank to see what came next.

"Now pick up the bridle. I'll tell you how to put it on the horse."

She did as she was told, her stomach fluttering. It took several tries to work the bit into the horse's mouth, but she finally learned to trust Moonbeam. They moved on to the remaining equipment, and in no time she had Moonbeam saddled.

She felt so proud when Moonbeam stood before her, ready to ride.

"Now unsaddle her."

She turned to Hank. "But…"

He gave her a steely stare.

"I thought I'd get to ride her, since she's all saddled."

"You're not ready yet."

She stared him down, but in the end she followed his instructions. He was, after all, the expert. She unsaddled the horse, and when she finished, she looked at Hank, a challenge in her eyes.

"Good," he replied, without any expression. Then he said, "Now saddle her again."

She waited for him to say what to put on the horse.

"Without my help," he said.

She prayed she could remember the order of what she'd done only a few minutes before, and was pleased with herself when she got it right.

Hank offered no words of praise. Nor did he tell her to unsaddle Moonbeam again, as she'd expected.

"Now mount up."

Feeling a rush of adrenaline, she stepped up to the side of Moonbeam, wondering how she was supposed to climb onto such a tall animal.

Hank's sharp words stopped her.

"You're on the wrong side of the horse. You need to be on her left side. That's the way most horses are trained."

"Oh, sorry, Moonbeam." She started to walk behind her to the other side.

"Don't go around the back of the horse. Go around the front so she can see you. Some horses kick when you go behind them."

Nervous now, Andrea walked around the front of the mare and moved to the left stirrup. She paused, trying to figure out which foot went in first.

"Your left!" Hank barked.

She glared at him. Did he have to yell? And why didn't he just explain all these rules before?

She put her left foot in the stirrup and using all her strength, swung her other leg over the horse. Much to her surprise, her body settled into the saddle as if it belonged there.

"Good job. Now dismount."

She considered taking the right side to dismount, but Hank told her, "Left side!"

She slid off the horse on the left side. She figured he would tell her to mount up again and she wasn't disappointed. She swung up into the saddle once more, a bit more smoothly this time, and hoped he'd let her stay there and begin teaching her to ride. But alas, no. He ordered her to dismount, then turned on his heel to leave.

"Unsaddle her and then you can amuse yourself till lunch." With that he simply walked out of the barn.

Andrea rested her head against Moonbeam's long neck and stifled a scream.

"Honestly, Jessica, all I did was saddle and unsaddle Moonbeam. I thought he'd let me ride a little bit, at least. I was so frustrated!"

"I guess you were, but you have to know how to take care of your horse. You did say you wanted to learn to ride like a cowboy, didn't you?"

"Yes, but I didn't think Hank would be so…formal!"

The man himself stepped into the kitchen. "If you don't like my teaching techniques, Miss Jacobs, we'll be glad to refund you your money, except for the cost of the food and lodging we've provided so far, and you can go elsewhere."

The kitchen was painfully silent for several moments.

Then Andrea spoke. "I didn't mean to be so harsh, *Mr. Ledbetter.* I just thought I might be allowed to ride a little bit."

"If you can manage to saddle your horse properly after lunch, you'll be allowed to ride this afternoon."

"Really? Why didn't you tell me that this morning?"

"I don't think it's necessary to inform my students of every step when I'm teaching them."

Jessica stepped between them. "But you could change your rules slightly, Hank. That wouldn't be so hard, would it?"

"Fine! When's lunch going to be ready?"

"I'm just getting ready to serve it. I'll put it on the table if you'll both be seated."

"You can have Jim's seat by Jess," Hank said to Andrea. "He won't be here." After saying that, Hank sat down on his side of the table.

With a shrug, Andrea sat down beside Jessica.

Jessica put another casserole on the table with a salad and some baked beans.

Andrea now understood the remark Hank had made to her at The Prime Rib about eating everything in front of her. She was starving.

When Jessica uncovered the dish, Andrea drew a deep breath. Then she looked up straight into Hank's eyes, noting the laughter there. At least he wasn't frowning. "Yes, you were right," she said with a chuckle.

"Good," Jessica said. "It's chicken pot pie. Be sure to fill your plate. And we have dessert, too."

"Oh, my, I don't know if I can eat that much."

"You can," Hank said.

She glared at him, but it was a wasted effort. He was already digging into his lunch. Which reminded her she was wasting time.

THE AFTERNOON LESSON went much better. After she successfully saddled Moonbeam, Hank told her to lead the mare out into the corral. She eagerly did so, waiting for the chance to ride for the first time ever. Hank didn't bring out a horse for himself, and that surprised her. He was going to let her ride alone?

He sauntered out into the corral and climbed onto the split-rail fence. "Now, lead her around for a while."

She thought about complaining, but she remembered what Jessica had told her about this morning's lesson. She'd better hold back. Maybe he really was trying to teach her to ride the cowboy way.

After half an hour, he drawled, "Okay, bring her over here and mount up. Remember, left side, left foot. When you step up into the saddle, swing your right foot over and into the right stirrup." While he was saying that, he got down from the fence and grabbed the horse's reins.

Oddly, there was something different about mounting the horse in the wide-open space of the corral, instead of in the barn. She felt anxious. "She won't run away, will she?"

"I'll hold her. Don't worry."

She gave him a tight smile. "I won't."

She put her left foot in the stirrup and tried to swing up, but she got caught, unable to pull her body up into the saddle. Suddenly she felt Hank's hands on her behind pushing her up. She gasped and nearly lost her grip on the horn. Her skin burned where he touched her. Somehow she found herself in the saddle.

"Sometimes dudes get caught in the middle."

Andrea felt her cheeks heat, not because he called her a "dude"—which, as an inexperienced rider, she supposed she was—but because she couldn't look him in the eye after he'd had his hands on her rear end.

True to form, though, he irritated her with his next words.

"Okay, ride her around the corral for a while. Remember, she'll do what you tell her with the reins. Pull gently left or right, and when you need to stop, pull back gently on both reins."

"You want me to ride in circles like a child?" she demanded.

"Yeah," Hank responded.

"But what about riding somewhere?"

Hank sighed and shook his head. "Just do what I say. You'll get there before you know it."

"Today?"

"Nope. But maybe tomorrow. It depends."

"On what?"

"On how quickly you recover."

She gave him a glare and started riding around the circle with her teeth gritted and in total silence. She wanted to prove that she could wait him out. After a few minutes, he shouted for her to stop. She pulled back on both reins. The horse was wonderfully responsive.

"Good. Now do a figure eight."

She rode the horse in a figure eight, enjoying that more than riding in a circle. Then he told her to reverse the figure eight.

He kept her going for a couple of hours, alternating the routine. When he finally brought her to a stop, he studied her. "How are you feeling?"

She was hurting a little, but she thought she could still ride. "I'm perfectly fine."

"No problems at all?"

After debating her answer, she finally said, "I'm a little sore."

"Okay, get down."

She tried to get down the way she'd gotten up, but her legs seemed to crumple under her. Before she knew it, Hank was holding her.

"Easy, Andrea. Give yourself a chance to get your legs back under you."

"What happened? I—I can hardly stand."

"Take it slow. You'll get the feeling back in a minute."

She didn't like his arms around her, his chest near her face, but she was afraid she'd fall to the ground if he let her go. She felt suddenly parched and her skin tingled.

Then he said, "You get a break because I'm going to unsaddle Moonbeam for you while you go up to the house. If you want a snack or something to make you feel better, just tell Jess."

"Okay, but how do I walk out of here?" She still couldn't trust her legs.

He led her to the gate, his arm still around her and holding her against the long, lean length of him. In spite of his going very slowly, she almost felt like asking him to carry her, but she wouldn't give in to that urge.

When he got her out of the corral, he asked, "Can you make it from here?"

She wanted to say yes, but her legs were still wobbly. "I—I think I can make it."

He shook his head and scooped her off her feet. "Never mind. I'll take you into the kitchen."

She didn't say anything. She was afraid he'd put her down.

When he got to the kitchen, he lowered her onto a chair.

Andrea could barely get words past her dry throat, but she pulled herself together enough to say, "Thank you, Hank."

"No problem." But he continued to lean over her, his face entirely too close.

She noticed for the first time how great he smelled. The outdoors, the crispness of the weather, the scent of leather. All infused her senses.

Hank looked her right in the eye and she could've sworn she saw a hint of a smile on his mouth.

But he pulled back quickly and made for the door. "Tell Jess not to count on me for dinner." He threw the words over his shoulder. "I'm going into town."

Andrea was surprised by how disappointed she felt.

AMAZING. HER MUSCLES felt so much looser after she'd soaked in the Epsom-salts bath. She didn't want to get out of the tub, but hunger pains drove her. She stood and reached for a fluffy towel. Sighing, she ran the towel over her body. She was tempted to crawl into bed, but she needed that steak Jessica was making.

Besides, if she didn't show for dinner, Hank might hear about it and think he'd managed to win the contest.

She pulled up short. Contest? Why did she seem to want to best him all the time, as if she needed to prove herself? She had every right to be the student, to be sore, to be a "dude." There was no harm in that. After all, she was out here to learn.

But there was something about Hank....

Somehow she felt she always needed to be on guard around him, to put up a strong facade—or else he'd see the weak, vulnerable woman underneath.

The woman who kept a secret.

The woman who could fall for him.

She stopped herself right there. That line of thinking could do no good, so she quickly dressed and went downstairs, limping only slightly.

She found Jessica already putting dinner on the table.

"I'm not late, am I?" she asked with a hesitant smile.

Jessica turned around. "I was just about to see how you were doing. I'm glad you made it down."

"Those special bath salts you gave me are miraculous. Thanks. I thought I'd never walk again when I first got off Moonbeam."

Jessica laughed. "Well, I think you did very well."

"Can I help with anything?"

"No, this is easy. Wait until you see the kitchen function when we have a full house."

"I'm sure it's a lot of work, but I bet it's fun, too."

"Actually, it has been fun—ever since Jim got here."

"I guess so, since you married him," Andrea said with a laugh.

"Oh, yes, that made it fun, but more importantly, he took care of my problems with my brothers. After our parents died and I got the idea of opening a dude ranch, Hank and Pete thought they could overrule me. Anything I wanted to do, they said no. It was a mess!"

"That must've been difficult."

"Aw, she's just teasing. They wanted to do everything she said," a deep voice said behind the two women.

Jim smiled at them when they faced him. "Well, maybe there *was* a little friction," he said as his wife stepped into his ready arms.

Jim stole a quick kiss and as Andrea watched the two of them, so obviously in love, she felt lonesome for the first time in her life.

When Jim let go of his wife, he said to Andrea, "Glad to see you're still able to walk."

"Yes, thanks to the Epsom salts."

"Hank worked you hard, I guess." He looked around the kitchen. "Where is he, anyway?"

"Hank said he was going into town," Andrea explained, remembering that moment with him earlier in the kitchen.

Jim frowned. "I wanted to talk to him."

Andrea knew what he meant. Once again she felt a rush of disappointment.

Chapter Four

When Andrea arrived at the barn the next morning, she found Hank engaged in a quiet but serious conversation with Jim. Noticing a hard look on Hank's face, she gave them some privacy and moved to the corral.

Did he ever smile?

Then she recalled his near-smile yesterday in the kitchen and her own racing heartbeat. Maybe it was a good thing he didn't smile. The effect of it could be devastating. At the very least, it was distracting.

And she could not afford to be distracted. She was here to accomplish one goal and one goal only.

She'd best keep her mind on that and off Hank Ledbetter.

She hitched her foot on a fence rail and looked around the ranch. Nestled in the Rockies, the Lazy L was everything its advertising brochure said it was. Quite a difference from the concrete canyons of New York City where she'd been raised and lived.

She loved the city; it was all she knew. The constant motion, the sounds, the energy. But there was no denying the natural beauty of Colorado.

But for a twist of fate, she realized, this could have been her home.

Before she could give that bit of irony much thought, Jessica sidled up to her.

"Did you hear any of their conversation?" she asked, nodding her head toward the barn. The frown on her face concerned Andrea.

She shook her head. "Is something wrong?"

"I'm not sure. Last night I asked Jim what he had to talk to Hank about, but he wouldn't say. I got the impression it was important, though."

Just then, the two men came out of the barn.

Andrea could read nothing on Hank's expression, but Jim eyed his wife closely.

"I own this ranch, too, you know," Jessica told him, rising to her full height. "If something's wrong, I need to know."

"Relax, Jess," her husband assured her. "Everything's fine. It's just guy talk."

Jessica didn't look as though she bought that excuse. Neither did Andrea.

Somehow she couldn't picture Hank casually making guy talk.

The cowboy in question turned to her then. "We ridin' today?"

"Yes, I'm riding."

"Well, then, let's go." Hank walked into the barn and Andrea hurried after him, even though she wanted to hear what Jim might say to Jessica.

When she entered the barn, Hank said, "Are you sore this morning?"

"No, not really." At his skeptical look, she back-tracked. "Well, maybe a little, but I think I can handle it."

"Good. We're going to take a ride this morning."

Shocked by his words, she almost stumbled. "We are?"

"Didn't you want to ride in the pasture yesterday?"

"Yes, but I didn't think... I mean, you acted like that wouldn't happen for weeks."

"Don't be silly. You're only going to be here for a month."

She looked at the man who'd growled at her yesterday. Why was he being so congenial this morning? Did it have anything to do with what Jim had told him?

In the barn, he tossed her Moonbeam's bridle. "Go into the pasture and find your horse. Bridle her there and lead her back to the barn."

"Okay," she said, not sure how she would catch Moonbeam. But she wasn't going to refuse.

Entering the pasture, she saw Moonbeam at once. Her distinctive coloring gave her away. Andrea slowly walked to the mare, coaxing her with soft words. Moonbeam actually took a few steps toward her, much to Andrea's surprise. She reached out to stroke the horse's neck.

"Good girl. Thank you for being so nice." Andrea got the bridle in place, then asked, "Are you ready? Want to come back to the barn with me?" She turned and led Moonbeam to the barn.

When she found Hank already saddling his horse, she exclaimed, "She came to me! Isn't that great?"

"I thought she would. Hurry up and saddle her. We're running behind."

"For what?"

"For what I have planned this morning."

She did as he said, but she felt something was up.

He swung into his saddle, watching her from atop his horse. When she finished saddling Moonbeam, he said, "Okay. Mount up. And remember I'm not there to catch you this time if you don't make it."

She gritted her teeth, afraid his reminder would jinx her. But she actually managed to get in the saddle the first time. She said breathlessly, "Okay, I'm ready."

"We're going to ride at a lope. Once you get your horse in that stride, you'll find it's easier than some of the other strides. If it's too much for you, let me know."

She was determined she wouldn't complain. She followed him out of the barn and he started across the pasture, moving much faster than she expected. Moonbeam seemed to assume she wanted to go that fast, too.

Much to her surprise, after a moment of gripping the saddle horn for dear life, she discovered a natural rhythm and her body adjusted. Though she didn't let go of the horn, she did relax a bit.

She was amazed at how much ground they were covering. It seemed everything was rushing up to meet them. When they reached the tree line, Hank pulled to a halt. Andrea's horse stopped abruptly—Moonbeam's choice, not hers.

"You okay?" Hank said.

"Yes," she replied, though she really wasn't.

"You did that well. Good girl."

Before she could delight in his praise, he was already moving forward again. Thankfully, it was at a much slower pace. She followed, deciding to file Hank's praise under "Rare and Unusual."

After a while, Hank stopped and swung down from his saddle, catching her by surprise. "Stay put. I'm just opening a gate."

After he pulled open the gate made of barbed wire and posts, he indicated she should ride through. He pulled his horse through and then fastened the gate behind them.

Back in his saddle, Hank checked her again. "Ready to go?"

"Yes. Are we going fast again?" She had to admit the speed had given her a rush.

"Honey, that wasn't fast, but yes, we're going to lope again." Then he actually chuckled.

She thought she'd never hear that sound from him. Now she understood what those women in Steamboat Springs saw in Hank. He was downright handsome. Sexy.

They crossed another pasture and another gate. She didn't realize how high they were until she looked back toward the house. The enormous Lazy L spread looked like a miniature from up here.

"It's a long way to the house," she said.

"Are you getting tired?"

"Maybe a little."

"We're almost there."

"Where?"

"Where we're going." He started off again, and she had no choice but to follow him.

When he pulled up the next time, he dismounted and came to her side. "Okay, slide down. I'll make sure you land on your feet."

She did as he said and was glad he was there to catch her. She dropped her reins as she put her hands on his shoulders. "I forgot my reins."

"Doesn't matter. Moonbeam is trained to stop when the reins fall." Then he swung her up into his arms.

"I think I can walk." She protested, but was forced to admit that Hank's arms felt wonderful. Strong and muscular, they cradled her under her legs and around her back, stirring up heat wherever they made contact. Her own arms locked around his neck, and she fought the urge to take off his hat and run her hands through his hair.

All too soon he put her down. She felt chilled.

"I want you to sit down here on this tree stump. Just wait a few minutes until I come back."

"Where are you going?"

"Just over here." He walked toward a group of trees.

Andrea strained to see what he was looking at. But she really couldn't tell much. Maybe there was a corral among the trees.

She told herself she should trust Hank. Then again, she couldn't trust him totally. Despite his pleasant disposition today, she had to remember he was still the same cowboy who'd made her angrier than her mother ever had. She laughed to herself. That was saying something!

After a few minutes, she struggled to her feet and walked toward him on wobbly legs. Calling to him, she saw him jerk back. The anger she glimpsed on his face disappeared as he walked over to her.

"Rested already?" he asked, as if she hadn't interrupted him.

"What is it, Hank? What did you find?"

"Nothing. I just thought this would be a good ride for you."

"I don't believe you."

"Hasn't it been good so far? You seemed to be enjoying yourself from what I saw." He grabbed his horse's reins. "Ready to go back?"

"Maybe," she finally said.

"Okay, let's mount up."

She gathered her reins and tried to swing into the saddle. She'd wondered why Hank hadn't mounted, but then was glad he hadn't so he could push her onto her saddle. Otherwise, she wouldn't have made it.

By the time they got back to the stables, she wasn't sure if she was worse off or better off than yesterday. When Hank helped her dismount, she breathed a sigh of relief.

He carried her into the kitchen again, where Jessica was standing at the sink. When he deposited her in a chair, he looked at her and murmured, "Good girl. You did great today. You can have the afternoon off."

He was gone before she could say thanks. She could only stare at the back door as it swung shut.

"What was that all about?" Jessica looked at her in puzzlement.

"We took a ride today and I did well, I guess. He gave me the afternoon off."

Jessica glanced at the door. "Odd that he didn't ask about lunch. Where'd he run off to?"

Andrea shrugged. "Chores, I guess."

"I wonder if it has anything to do with what Jim told him this morning."

Andrea sat quietly, waiting for the feeling to return to her legs, while her hostess worked in the kitchen.

Jessica asked a few questions about the ride, making conversation. "Where'd you ride? Out in the pasture?"

"Not just one. I think we rode through three pastures. We went quite high. The view of the house from up there was incredible."

Jessica put down the utensil and turned to Andrea, her expression solemn. "Were you north or south of the house?"

"North, I think."

"What did Hank tell you about where you were going?"

"He didn't tell me anything. When we reached our destination, he set me down on a stump to rest, and he walked off into a clump of trees."

"Could you tell what he was looking at?"

"Not really. When I got up to join him, he immediately came toward me before I could see anything exactly. I thought there might be some kind of rough corral, but I wasn't sure."

While she was talking, Jessica's expression turned downright angry.

"What is it, Jessica?"

"It means someone is stealing cattle. There's a small road just on the other side of the trees you saw."

"You mean we could've *driven* up there?" Andrea asked in exasperation.

"I wonder who he and Jim suspect."

"We didn't see anyone."

"No, Hank will take care of this now, this afternoon. You see, he knew you wouldn't want to ride more after a whole morning in the saddle."

"Well, he was right about that," Andrea said. "I think I may need help just getting out of this chair!"

IT HAD BEEN a long day, Hank thought as he returned to the ranch house later that night. A long and difficult day.

He knew Jim felt the same way. He dragged himself in alongside Hank. When they opened the door, Jessica was there to confront them.

"So who did you fire?"

Hank pulled up short and glanced at his brother-in-law. "What are you talking about?" he asked, a sick feeling in his stomach.

"I'm talking about the little corral you found hidden in the north pasture. The one that someone was using to rip us off."

Jim cursed, and Hank ran a hand through his hair. "Look, Jess—"

"Should I leave the room?"

Just then Hank noticed Andrea sitting at the kitchen table. She looked uneasy.

"No, of course not," Jessica said, smiling at her.

"Nah, you might as well join us. After all, I'm guessing it was your information that clued Jessie in," Hank said. "I didn't realize you saw so much."

"I didn't know what it meant." Andrea looked at Jessica.

"It's all right, Andrea. I shouldn't be having to guess."

Jim went to her, but she pushed his hands away. "Honey, I wasn't sure until Hank looked things over. I didn't want to worry you for nothing."

"So you were planning to tell me this evening?"

He looked at Hank. "Uh, yeah. Yeah, that's what I planned to do."

Jessie didn't fall for it and she let Jim have it.

Hank stepped between them and looked at his brother-in-law. "Damn it, Jim, why don't you tell her it's none of her business!"

Jim shook his head. "One day you'll be married and you'll understand why."

"I don't think so!" Hank exclaimed in disgust. "I'm never getting married!"

He didn't know what was worse. Jim having to kowtow to his wife or the thought of himself chained to a wife. Either way, it was distasteful.

He grabbed a glass of water and sat down.

"Not sure I should even ask this question, but what happened on the ranch?" Andrea asked.

Hank looked at her. It wasn't her fault, he realized. She'd no doubt only answered the questions his sister had asked, and Jess was one smart cowgirl. "A couple of our cowboys were stealing a few cows and selling them for slaughter," he explained. "We might not've caught them if they hadn't taken one of the nursing mothers. We noticed the orphaned calf."

Andrea looked upset.

"Don't worry, the calf's okay." A typical city-girl reaction, he thought with a snicker.

And a typical Andrea reaction, something inside him added. Her soft heart *would* have her worrying about the calf.

Despite all his bravado, Hank had to admit that the Andrea he was spending time with wasn't at all what he'd expected from a New York socialite. She had held her own—and she'd done so with grace.

"I'm sorry I couldn't tell you," he said to her and to Jess. "But I needed to see the place Jim was talking about before I confronted the ones who were guilty."

"How could you tell who they were?"

"I didn't know by looking at the corral. I made some phone calls. When I found the slaughterhouse that had taken in the cows, I threatened to have them shut down if they didn't describe the two men who brought the cows in. Then I knew."

"Did you fire them?" Jessica asked in a hard voice.

Jim answered. "Yeah, we did. They left this after-noon."

"Good. We don't want anyone thinking we don't care about our herd just because we're operating a dude ranch."

"I think we made that clear," Hank said.

Andrea looked at him. "Do those two riders have a place to stay tonight?"

"We didn't ask them."

"But they may not—"

"Andrea, once they've stolen cattle, they're on their own," Hank said. "We don't worry about them anymore."

"I guess I'm being silly. But it just seems harsh to—"

"Yeah, well, we're pretty harsh when someone steals from us."

Andrea ducked her head after that.

"Who were they?" Jessica asked.

"Billy and Steve," Jim said.

"Steve? The one who entertained the guests last season?" Jessica asked. "He was such a good singer."

"Yeah. He was making extra money from us for singing, and he was still stealing our cows," Hank said.

Jessica filled Andrea in on how Steve played the guitar and sang some nights for the dude-ranch guests.

"Can you find someone else?" she asked Jess.

"We'll have to, I guess," Jessica said, frowning.

"We'll look around for someone, honey, don't worry."

"I don't see how. Are you going to ask the ones you're thinking about hiring to sing for their job?" Jessica asked.

"Let's start with our own cowboys," Hank suggested. "There might be somebody else who can play guitar and sing."

"But wouldn't they have volunteered with Steve?"

Hank shook his head. "Not necessarily. Cowboys are basically shy. You should know that."

Andrea looked at him then. "Shy? Really?"

"Sure," Hank said.

"But you're a cowboy, aren't you?"

Chapter Five

Hank wasn't shy, and he was proud of it. Nobody got anything in life by being afraid of his own shadow. You had to work for what you wanted out of life. And if that made him bold, so be it.

He waited until Jim and Jessica stopped laughing before he told Andrea, "Yes, I'm a cowboy, but I'm also a ranch owner. That makes the difference."

"I see," Andrea said, hiding a smirk herself.

"Well, Hank, seeing as how you're not shy—" his sister cleared her throat in emphasis "—would you go to the bunkhouse and ask the cowboys if any of them can sing and play guitar?" Jessica turned serious. "I really need to get a singer lined up. We've got guests scheduled to arrive in a few weeks."

Hank shook his head. "I was going to head into town."

"Surely you'll help your sister tonight," Andrea said. "After all, you went into town once already this week."

"I wasn't aware you were keeping tabs on me," he told her with a suspicious leer.

"Yeah, Hank, you can skip going into town tonight, can't you?" Jessica pleaded.

Hank knew he owed his sister his support because of his uncooperative behavior when they first started the dude ranch. Still, he was reluctant to give in.

"I'd go with you," Jim said, "but I've got some... chores to do around the house. Namely making up with my wife." He looked at Jess and grinned.

Before Hank could relent, Andrea spoke up. "I can come with you, Hank."

Now that sounded like a good idea.

"Okay, but let's go now. The sooner we find some-one, the sooner I can go to town."

"I don't think you'll find someone that fast," Jessica said, "because you'll have to bring him up here to let me hear him."

"He won't do that!" Hank protested.

"Why not?"

"Because, like I said, cowboys are shy."

"Oh, please! Look, Jim and I will set up in the living room. I'll even fix some snacks. That will be enough to tempt him."

"It might work, Hank," Jim said softly. "You know how a workingman likes to eat."

"Fine!" He got up to go to the bunkhouse, then stopped and looked at Andrea. "Aren't you coming?"

She got up. "Let's go enlist a singer or two." She grabbed her jacket and followed Hank out.

The November night had turned sharply colder and Hank could see his breath when he spoke.

"Why'd you offer to come with me?"

She seemed to hesitate before she replied. "I—I just wanted to help out Jessica."

"Really?" he asked. "Or did you not want me to go to town?"

She looked at him, her face innocent. "Why would that matter to me?"

He tried to read her eyes but couldn't. He shrugged. "No reason."

They walked to the bunkhouse and Hank suggested she wait outside until he made sure the men were dressed and decent. The bunkhouse wasn't usually a place for a woman.

Some of the cowboys were eating dinner when he entered, while others lounged around, enjoying their time off. None of them seemed too happy to see him.

"Something wrong, boss?" one of the men asked, rising to his feet.

"Nah. I'm here on behalf of Jessica. In light of the…firings today, it seems we no longer have a singer for the guests come December. Jessica wants to know if any of y'all can sing worth a damn."

The cowboys looked around one another. The silence stretched for a while until one by one a few men stepped forward.

Hank couldn't believe it. "Well, get yourselves all presentable and come up to the house. Jessica wants to hear you sing."

The guys groaned.

"Now, go on," Hank ordered. "I'll wait outside for you so you don't change your minds."

Scratching his head, he went outside to Andrea and told her the good news.

"Either these guys are singing to the coyotes or a lot

more goes on in that bunkhouse than I know." He couldn't help but laugh. A deep belly laugh that felt so good.

He noticed Andrea staring at him. "What is it?" he asked. "You don't think this is funny?"

"It's not that. I've just never seen you laugh before. You should do more of it. It becomes you."

"Oh, really? How so?"

She looked away. "No reason."

He reached out his hand and turned her face back to him. "Tell me."

In the light from the bunkhouse he could see her eyes clearly now. They were blue, he noticed for the first time. And not for the first time, he could see how beautiful she was. Fresh-faced, with perfect cheekbones and full lips. Lips he suddenly felt the urge to kiss.

"When you smile or laugh, your face lights up," she said softly, tentatively. "But you're always so serious. Laugh more. You're handsome when you do."

"Am I handsome now?" he asked, giving her a hint of a smile.

She averted her eyes.

"I'll take that as a yes."

He could feel Andrea shiver. "Are you cold? I told the guys we'd wait for them. I was afraid they'd chicken out."

Like he'd chickened out? More than anything he wanted to kiss this woman, to take her in his arms and surrender to the tension he felt around her since the first day he met her at the airport. But something was holding him back.

He couldn't quite put his finger on it.

Andrea shivered again and he pulled her behind the bunkhouse, using it to shield the wind that rolled down from the mountains. He hitched himself up on the fence and put his arm around her to warm her.

"Can I ask you something, Hank?"

"Of course," he replied.

"Why are you so dead set against marriage?"

The unexpected question hit him upside the head. "Excuse me?"

She pulled away from his arm and looked at him. "Before, at the house, you practically screamed at Jim when he said one day you'd know what it'd be like to be married. You made it sound like a fate worse than death."

Hank took off his hat and ran his hand through his hair. "I... Getting married isn't for me."

"According to Jessica, your parents had a great marriage. And she seems to be happy. Why would you—"

"Because I'm just not interested, that's all." Though he tried to keep the harshness out of his voice, Andrea looked taken aback. "Listen, Andrea," he explained, "there's no deep-seated psychological reason for it. I just like being a bachelor. I like women."

One, in particular, a voice said in his head.

"I can see that." And then Andrea crossed her arms over her breasts and turned away. "Why don't you move those cowboys along so we can get this over with? Wouldn't want them stopping you from going to town."

Now she was mad at him.

He reached out for her, but the bunkhouse door opened and a rowdy group of cowboys emerged.

"Speak of the devil," he said. "Let's go."

JESSICA AND JIM were sitting in the living room when Hank led the cowboys in.

"Looks like you got lucky, Jess. We got a few volunteers to audition," Hank said as he stepped through the doors. "I told them they'd get something to eat even if you *don't* choose them."

"That's right. Come on in, gentlemen." She ushered the cowboys into seats. "Don't be shy. We're all family."

"*She* ain't," one of the younger cowboys said, nodding at Andrea.

Jessica gave Hank a look that chastised him for not introducing their guest. "This is Andrea Jacobs. She's Hank's riding pupil."

The men didn't hesitate to introduce themselves to Andrea, who graciously greeted them. A little too graciously, in Hank's opinion.

"Come on, guys, you didn't come here to meet Andrea. You're supposed to sing for Jess." Hank moved them away from Andrea and sat down beside her.

A quartet stood up and sang together, sounding remarkably well rehearsed.

"That was wonderful," Jessica praised them. "Is there anyone else?"

"Yeah," Hank replied when the cowboys sat quietly. "Slim, bring your guitar and get on up there."

In his pure tenor, Slim sang a Christmas song, accompanying himself on his guitar.

"I had no idea we had such talent!" Jessica enthused. She told the cowboys what she would pay for their singing and guitar playing, in addition to the salary they got as cowpunchers, and the men seemed pleased. She thanked them for coming.

"Don't forget the treats," Hank told her in a stage whisper.

"Oh, yes, and we'd love for you to stay for some refreshments."

When the men had their plates full, Hank solicited Jim's help to fetch drinks for everyone. He couldn't help but notice that a few of the cowboys had huddled around Andrea. Slim, in particular, sidled up to her with his best Sunday manners.

And Andrea looked happy to be the center of attention. She smiled at them, laughed at their jokes and poured on the charm.

And Hank stewed.

"I'm glad I married Jess," Jim whispered to Hank with a chuckle. "At least I know she's safe from the cowboys."

Hank didn't laugh.

HANK STILL SEEMED in a bad mood.

As Andrea stepped into the horse barn, he barely mumbled a good-morning. She didn't understand why he'd turned sour last night. Everyone had been having such a good time, listening to the cowboys sing, laughing and mingling. Except Hank. He stood off by himself, and if she wasn't mistaken, he glared at her.

The same way he was glaring at her now.

Too bad. She was in a happy mood. It was a beautiful day and she had riding to look forward to.

But Hank would barely speak to her.

"Aren't we going to ride?" she asked him.

"You're paying for it," he said, grabbing his tack. "Saddle up. You remember how?"

"Of course I do." Methodically she saddled Moonbeam, doing everything exactly the way he'd taught her.

She hoisted herself into the saddle at the same time Hank did.

Side by side they rode out into the pasture.

"Nice day, isn't it?" Andrea said when the silence got deafening.

"Yeah."

After a few minutes she tried again. "I saw the sunrise this morning. For the first time in my life."

"Good for you."

His terse answers were beginning to annoy her.

"Hank, are you mad at me for some reason?"

"No."

"Then why won't you talk to me?" She didn't want to plead with him. She merely wanted some companionship.

He said nothing for a while, then finally relented. "Didn't figure you for an early riser."

"Guess I'm still on New York time." Her body clock might still be confused, but she absolutely loved Colorado. It was beautiful here, and she found she missed the noise and energy of the city less each day. "I went down to help Jessica with breakfast. Didn't you eat this morning? I didn't see you."

"I got an early start." He paused, then said, "You know, you're paying good money for riding lessons. You don't have to ingratiate yourself with me by helping my sister in the kitchen."

"I don't mind. And I'm not 'ingratiating' myself." His sour mood was beginning to rub off.

"Well, Mary Jo will be back soon and she'll run you both out of the kitchen."

"Whatever." Now she was the one with the terse, one-word answers.

OVER THE NEXT TEN days or so, Andrea and Hank went out riding every morning, and sometimes the lessons went on into the afternoon. Her skills were improving, and she was pleased to note that she wasn't so sore and stiff anymore. Hank was a great teacher, but he rarely said much, obviously preferring to keep their conversation on a professional level. She did learn a lot about horses, though.

Today, they had saddled up and were just starting the day's lesson. "What's the plan for riding today? Will I have the afternoon off?" Andrea asked.

"Why?"

"Jessica's going into town to buy Christmas decorations for the house. I thought it would be nice to go with her."

Hank stared at Andrea. "I thought you wanted to learn to ride!"

"I do, but…but I love Christmas decorations."

"Don't you have some of your own to put up when you get back home?"

"Not really." She leaned down to stroke Moonbeam's neck, suddenly uneasy with Hank's line of questioning and his assessing look.

"You've got the money. Buy some."

"It's not that simple. You see, my mother usually hires a decorating company to come out and put up our tree. It's silver, not a real tree. I've never gotten to choose anything for Christmas."

Realizing she sounded like a spoiled little rich girl, she stopped herself. "I'm sorry. I didn't mean to go off like that."

Hank shrugged. "I guess we could ride only half a day. But we can't do this all the time. You'll never learn that way." He shot her a stern look.

She smiled. "Thanks, Hank. Jessica will be happy, too."

"You really enjoy doing things with Jess?"

"Yes. We get along well. We seem to like the same things."

"How can that be? You grew up in New York."

"I know. But we do."

"Hmm. You seem to like the ranch, too. Or I'm not so sure about that. Maybe you just like being around cowboys who flirt with you."

"What!" Against her will, color flared in her cheeks. "Just because the cowboys on the ranch nod and say hello to me does not mean they're flirting!"

"Trust me, I know men. And those men want you."

"You're being ridiculous. They're just polite, that's all." Besides, she wasn't interested in any of the good-looking young cowboys. Only one cowboy at the Lazy L interested her—and he was riding beside her.

"Just be careful."

She turned to stare at him, taking her eyes off the trail. "Is that a warning, Hank?"

"Take it any way you want." He nickered to his horse and picked up the pace.

She kept up with him, moving easily into a faster gait.

When she pulled up alongside him again, she almost thought he looked impressed.

"I think we should ride at a fast gallop, just for a couple of minutes, to see how you do. You see that pine tree up ahead?"

"Yes."

"I want you to kick your heels into Moonbeam and make her go as fast as she can. But hang on tight. And when you reach the tree, pull her to a stop."

Andrea was eager to show him what she could do, but she couldn't forget about safety. "Are you sure I can do this?"

"Yeah, you can, I'm sure. I want you to know just how fast your horse is, in case you ever need to get away from something."

"Like what?"

"A bear or something."

Her lungs felt devoid of air. "You have bears out here?"

"Not often, but sometimes during the summer, they come around."

Luckily she wouldn't be around for the summer.

"Ready?" he asked.

"Yeah."

She signaled Moonbeam, and horse and rider took off, Hank and his mount beside them. Her braid flew behind her and wind rushed into her face as the mare ate up the distance. In no time she made it to the pine tree.

"That was amazing!" she managed to get out when they stopped at the tree.

"Did you have any trouble staying on?"

"No. But I had to hold on to the saddle horn."

"That's all right. Now let's turn and lope back."

There wasn't any difficulty finding the right gait, because Moonbeam imitated Hank's horse. From there, Hank had her slow Moonbeam to a trot, and finally a walk.

When they were back at the barn, Hank swung down from his horse and came over to help her unsaddle Moonbeam. But Andrea was already out of the saddle. "I can do it, Hank. I've got my legs."

"You sure?"

"Yes, I'm sure."

They worked side by side till their horses were done.

Hank followed her back to the house for lunch. As they walked by the corral, they passed a couple of the cowboys who'd sung the other night. They called out to her and waved. She returned their greetings.

"You know," Hank said beside her, "I've been thinking. Maybe I'll go shopping with you and Jess."

Could he be more obvious? Andrea thought.

She stopped and turned toward him in an exaggerated motion, her hand going to her chest. "You? Shopping? I can't imagine it!"

Chapter Six

They went to the largest department store in Steamboat Springs to shop.

Jim had joined them, too, taking the afternoon off and leaving Slim in charge of the Lazy L—thanks to Hank's suggestion.

"I appreciate you telling me to come, Hank," Jim said as the foursome entered the enormous Christmas department, decorated gaudily for the holidays. There were dozens of artificial trees and thousands of bright lights vying for attention with piped-in carols and animated figures.

Andrea didn't know where to look first. This was the way she'd decorate the ranch if it were hers. Once the snow hit, the place would look like a winter wonderland.

She and Jessica dove right in, oohing and ahhing about everything they saw. The two men followed behind.

Jessica stopped to look at a giant fir tree. Jim stepped forward to his wife's side. "Why are you looking at this tree, honey? It's fake."

"I know, but I want to get a tree up right away, and I don't think we can keep it alive until New Year's. Maybe we can bring in some real tree branches several times to give the scent of Christmas. Besides, this tree will last for years."

"That's true. Okay, I like this one. It'll look great in the living room."

"You don't think it's too tall?"

"No, I don't. Let's get it."

"Okay." She waved to a saleswoman. "We want to buy this tree."

"This size?"

"Yup."

Andrea was thrilled. At least she'd get to see it put up and maybe even get to decorate it.

They spent the afternoon choosing different things to make the big ranch house look Christmassy. Jim found a massive wreath to hang on the front door. Hank found a Santa, sleigh and reindeer to set on the mantel. The women, after choosing sets of multicolored balls to hang on the tree, chose individual ornaments, as well. Andrea selected an arrangement of Old World angels in moiré and crystal. They were exactly what she'd use to decorate her own place. If she had her own place.

She thought of her mother's austere apartment back in New York. This year, with her mother and her husband gone abroad for the holiday, the place would be empty. Other years, though, the decorator had chosen a theme; no matter what it was, the color was always the same—silver. Cold and passionless, just like her mother. She looked down at the colorful ornaments in their basket. Reds, greens, plaids, tapestries—all of which her mother would have deemed "pedestrian."

Andrea decided that when she returned to New York, she'd start looking for her own apartment, one she could decorate exactly as she pleased. At twenty-four, she should have her own place, anyway. Her mother had gotten her own way long enough.

"Do you think we're buying too much?" Jessica's question broke into Andrea's thoughts.

"No, that tree is huge."

"I guess you're right. Besides, this is the first winter season we'll have guests at the ranch. If we want to make our reputation as the place to go for Christmas, we need to go all-out."

They continued to pick out ornaments until they realized the men were missing.

"Do you see them anywhere?" Andrea asked, her eyes scanning the store.

"No, and they're pretty tall. We should be able to see them." She craned her neck to search. "Where could they have gone?"

Suddenly they both saw them at once. "There they are, coming out of the dressing room!" Jessica said.

"What were they doing in the dressing room?" Andrea wondered aloud. First she'd somehow managed to get Hank to shop, and now he was trying on clothes? She laughed to herself. It was a Christmas miracle.

Jessica asked her husband when they approached.

"We were trying on Santa suits. We figure Pete, Hank and I wear about the same size, so we can take turns being Santa."

"How did they look?" Andrea asked Hank.

"Not bad. We just need to add stuffing," Hank said.

Without thinking, Andrea moved over and fastened one stray button on his shirt, right above his belt. She nearly gasped when she caught herself.

"Or eat more." She kept her eyes on his flat stomach, too embarrassed to look up and too enraptured to look away.

"I don't think I can eat that much—unless I stop working."

"Maybe you can have the day off when you play Santa," Andrea suggested.

"Yeah, right." Hank just shrugged.

"Wait a minute!" Jessica said, diverting her attention. "What is Santa going to deliver? We have no gifts!"

Jim hugged his wife. "We didn't mean to stress you out, honey. We thought you'd be pleased with all we've bought."

"I am, sweetheart. But we'll have to do a little more shopping—for gifts. I'll have to check and see how many adults and children we have coming for Christmas week."

"I'll help you wrap gifts," Andrea volunteered. Again, she couldn't help recalling the gifts she'd gotten as a child and now as an adult. Her mother usually just handed her a check.

"Thanks for offering, Andrea. I'm sure I'll be calling on you for help. There's a lot to get done before December first."

"Are you going to have a Christmas tree in each cottage?"

"I hadn't thought of that. Maybe we should cut down enough trees and decorate them for each cabin. That would be good, especially if there are children."

"Uh, ladies, I hate to interrupt…" Hank glanced down at his watch and rubbed his stomach. "My belly's getting empty and you know how I get when I'm hungry. Could we come back another time for those decorations? We don't have to do the cabin trees tonight."

Jim checked his watch, too. "I didn't realize it was this late. Hank's right. Let's arrange the delivery of everything we bought and then go have dinner."

"We can't have them deliver tonight," Jessica said, already steering for the saleswoman who'd helped them.

Once the woman scheduled the delivery for the first available time, Jessica returned to the others. "Okay, we can eat now. What do you suggest, Hank? I've heard about that hot new restaurant, Carousel. You know it, don't you?"

"Yeah, they serve good food there."

"And that's why you go there, isn't it?" Jim teased.

"Is that where he goes when he comes to town?" Andrea asked in a whisper to Jessica. "Where he meets women?"

Jessica nodded.

"Will we see some of those women tonight?"

Jessica nodded again.

"Don't you want to go there?" Hank asked Andrea.

She put up her hands in a defensive gesture. "I don't know any of the restaurants. It's your choice."

"Well, let's get a move on. We don't want to get caught up in their late rush," Jim said.

Carousel wasn't far from the department store, so they left their car and walked. The sidewalks were beginning to crowd with evening shoppers and diners, and Hank reached out his arm to take hold of Andrea as they swerved through the oncoming pedestrians. She told herself he was only being gentlemanly.

When they entered the Western-themed restaurant, Hank was greeted personally by the hostess, an attractive young woman. She immediately led them to a table.

A few cowboys gave Andrea some looks as she passed their table.

Hank pulled her closer. "Just ignore those cowboys. They aren't the shy ones," he murmured.

Andrea asked, "Are the women the shy ones?" She couldn't help noticing the interested looks coming Hank's way from a couple of young women at the bar.

Hank ignored her words, pulling out a chair at the table. Once they were all seated, Hank told them the best things on the menu.

Andrea was watching the women who were hovering in the background. They were looking at Hank as if they were starving and he was premium-grade beef.

"What are you going to order, Andrea?"

She realized Hank was speaking to her. "I'm sorry. I'm afraid I wasn't listening."

"What were you doing?" he asked suspiciously.

"I was watching those women." She nodded her head toward the twosome at the bar. "Are they friends of yours?"

Hank didn't even bother looking. "Yeah. But we need to order."

"What do you recommend?"

He gave her a frustrated look. "I just said what I think is good. Do you want me to repeat myself?"

"No, of course not. I'll take…" She paused as she scanned the menu. "I'll have a salad."

"Which one?" Hank demanded.

Jessica leaned across the table. "I'm having the chicken Caesar salad."

"I'll have that, too."

A waitress appeared at their table, greeting Hank by name. "Nice to see you. So you didn't come alone tonight." Hank and she made small talk, then she finally got around to taking their drink and appetizer orders.

Andrea was about to ask just how often Hank came here when the two women from the bar approached their table. One of them, a redhead, wrapped her arm around Hank's neck, real cozy. "Hank, we were hoping you'd show up tonight."

He stiffened. "Uh, yeah, hi. It's good to see both of you."

"Aren't you going to introduce us to your friends?"

"Oh, sure, this is my sister, Jessica, and her husband, Jim. And this is Andrea…a friend."

His sister looked at him. "Are you going to tell us their names?"

"Oh, yeah, this is Sondra and Callie."

Sondra, the redhead, leaned down and whispered in Hank's ear.

"Uh, no, I can't join you tonight."

"But you haven't been here in a couple of nights."

"Sorry, I'm busy right now." He pulled her arm from his neck gently and gave her an uneasy smile.

Sondra and the blonde she was with walked away, but not without longing looks at Hank.

"Sorry about that," Hank muttered.

Jim barely stifled a laugh and got a look from Jessica. Andrea couldn't help but comment, "Life's tough for you, I see."

"I didn't ask them to come over here," he retorted.

"They seem pretty…comfortable with you, I notice," she said, enjoying seeing Hank squirm.

Music from a live band started up just then, drowning out further conversation. Andrea suspected Hank was grateful for the reprieve. But he surprised her when he leaned in close and whispered in her ear, "Want to dance?"

She pulled back and looked at him, aghast. "I haven't danced in—" But Hank pulled her to her feet.

"What about when the drinks and appetizers come?" she asked, looking for any excuse.

"They can wait. It's just a dance." He wrapped his arm around her and pulled her to him.

She inhaled his aftershave and forgot to protest. All she could think about was his hand, splayed on the small of her back.

"Do you dance a lot?" she asked, looking to break the tension.

"Some. Why? Don't you dance in New York?" He spun her around. "Or am I doing it wrong?"

"You're very good. But I don't dance that often."

"You dance like you've been taught."

"I had dance lessons, of course. Ballet when I was little, modern and ballroom when I got older. But I didn't... I mean, I wasn't a debutante."

"Why not? I could see you dressed in a gown and going to a ball."

She laughed. "I'm not a princess, Hank. Besides, I don't like that whole scene. Those people aren't—" She bumped into another couple.

"Let's change partners, Hank," the man said, his gaze fixed on Andrea.

"No thanks, Barry," Hank replied calmly. Then he twirled Andrea around away from the couple.

That was when Andrea realized the woman was Lucy of the lavender hat, the woman from the store on Andrea's first night in Colorado. "Did you want to dance with Lucy? I don't mind if you do."

"I don't want to. Now, you were telling me why you weren't a debutante. Not enough money?" He pulled her close again, his hand tighter on her back.

The temperature in the restaurant seemed to rise. She suddenly needed some air. "No, that's not the reason. I just wasn't interested."

"I thought all girls liked going to parties."

"That's what my mother thought, too."

"Did she give you a hard time?"

She could recall each and every one of their arguments. Her mother demanded Andrea go, and Andrea just wanted to hang out at a local pub with her friends. "Yes, but I outlasted her."

Hank leaned back and studied her face, his expression serious. "I bet you would have been a beautiful debutante. And I bet all the young men were disappointed."

"Thank you." That was all she could get past her parched throat.

He glanced away. "I hate to admit it, but our appetizers just arrived at the table."

Thank God for Hank's appetite.

When they sat down again, Andrea noticed an odd look pass between Jessica and her husband. Jessica smiled, while Jim nodded.

Hank noticed, too. "What are you agreeing to, Jim?"

"Just married talk, Hank. You wouldn't understand."

The rest of the evening passed quickly, with more dancing, more drink and more food. Andrea couldn't remember the last time she'd had so much fun.

That was one of the reasons she'd been looking forward to this trip. But only one.

When they got home, it was late and Andrea excused herself.

"I'll walk you up," Hank offered. "I'm going to turn in myself. We've got an early day tomorrow."

He followed Andrea up and walked her to her door.

She stopped with her hand on the knob and turned to say good-night. Would Hank try to kiss her? Part of her hoped not, while the rest of her prayed he would.

He looked down at her and took a step forward, not saying anything. Inch by inch his mouth lowered until it stopped a mere whisper from hers. He parted his lips and Andrea was about to close her eyes and fall into his kiss when he said, "Sleep tight."

Then he walked down the hall to his room, leaving her standing there, agape and bereft.

"Sleep tight?" she echoed when she'd shut the door behind her? He'd gotten her all hot and bothered for "Sleep tight"?

She threw herself on the bed and sighed.

Just as well, said an inner voice. She had no business getting wrapped up in a cowboy when she was leaving in a couple of weeks. She had to cool things between them, keep it professional. After all, she was only here to *learn* from Hank. Not fall in love with him.

THE FOLLOWING MONDAY the tree was delivered, along with all the decorations.

When Andrea and Hank came in for lunch, Jessica was waiting for them.

"Are we going to put the tree together this evening?" Andrea asked her.

"Maybe. If Jim feels up to it."

"Just make him a good dessert and he'll do whatever you want," Hank suggested.

She laughed. "You sure you're not talking about yourself, brother of mine?"

"Well, if you ask me, I could go for some peach cobbler with ice cream."

"I'll see what I can do." Jessica changed the subject. "How are the riding lessons going, Andrea?"

"Great. We're riding all over the ranch now."

"Good for you. Are you planning on an overnight trip?"

Andrea looked puzzled, and she turned to Hank. "Are we?"

"We can if you want. It would be fun if Jessie and Jim could go with us."

Andrea looked back at Jessica. "Could you?"

"That would depend on Jim. If he trusts Slim to be in charge…or if Pete and Mary Jo get back before you leave."

"When are they due back?"

"End of next week, I think."

"We can wait until then, can't we, Hank?"

"As long as *you* can wait that long. But we have to take the trip before the guests start arriving."

"It sounds so exciting!"

"It was for Mary Jo." Jessica explained how Hank and Pete had taken Mary Jo out and had to wait out a freak snowstorm in a cave.

"We got her home safely, though," Hank said.

"Yeah, and lucky for her, because that's the reason she and Pete got back together," Jessica added.

"They broke up?"

"Yes, Pete was…well, he wasn't faithful."

"What do you mean?"

Hank put down his fork and wiped his mouth. "While they were dating, Pete slept with one of our guests."

"How…why did she forgive him?"

"He apologized," Hank said, as if that explained it all. Then he took a drink and continued, "And that's one of the reasons I'm never getting married. You have to give up your freedom."

WHEN THEY GOT IN from riding late that afternoon, Andrea went upstairs to take a shower and change.

She'd spent most of the afternoon thinking about

Hank's comment on marriage. He saw it as a form of bondage, of abdicating freedom. Little wonder why he wasn't eager to enter the institution. But marriage didn't have to be like that.

Not that her own parents had been the best example.

They'd split when Andrea was a little girl, her mom taking her to New York to live. Even her mother's second marriage was far from loving. To Andrea, it seemed more a convenient financial arrangement, with her mother getting richer. But Andrea still believed in love. Love, happily ever after and Mr. Right. He was still out there somewhere.

He just wasn't here on the Lazy L.

Good thing she learned Hank's true feelings now. She'd been on the verge of falling for him.

Then again, women probably fell for Hank all the time, if the women at the Carousel were any indication.

She remembered the two women who'd approached Hank that night. The redhead in the tight sweater and the blonde with the long, wavy tresses. As she dressed for the evening, she purposely chose a pretty sweater and matching slacks with those women in mind. Then she blew her hair dry and curled it, leaving it down and loose on her shoulders. Though she'd gone most of the month without makeup, tonight she wore it.

She had a mission tonight. She wanted to make a point to Hank. *She* wasn't going to tie him down! She just wanted to make him hungry!

WHEN HANK CAME IN for dinner, he went straight to the coffeepot. All day he'd been dragging, maybe because he hadn't slept well last night. In fact, he'd been restless since the night at the Carousel.

And it had all to do with Andrea.

He'd come so close to kissing her that night. At the last minute he'd backed off, catching himself and reminding himself that she was a guest. She was not one of his Steamboat Springs women. Quite the contrary, Andrea was the marrying kind of woman.

And he was not the marrying kind of man.

He'd since remembered that and kept his hands off. She was his pupil, nothing else.

The woman in question entered the kitchen as he sipped his coffee. He nearly spit it out when he saw her.

A tight red sweater showed off all her curves, and the hair she usually wore in a braid or ponytail fell loose around her shoulders, begging to be touched. His hands itched to reach out to her.

"Hank?"

How long had she been calling him? He felt like he was in a trance.

"Hank, are you all right?"

"I'm fine." He steadied himself and took another sip of coffee. "You look nice tonight," he said, trying for nonchalance.

"Thanks." She started to set the table, and every move enticed him even more. Her stretching up to retrieve the dishes in the cabinet, bending down to get glasses out of the dishwasher. She was killing him.

He reminded himself of his resolve, but it was hard to listen to reason.

He was never so happy to see Jim and Jessie come

in for dinner. He jumped up and pulled out Andrea's chair for her.

"Damn, Hank, you make me look like a boor," Jim said.

Jessie patted his leg. "It's okay, honey. You worked all day."

"Hey, *I* worked!" Hank said. "It's not easy keeping up with Andrea."

Andrea regarded him in annoyance. "Let me know if I'm working you too hard!"

"I didn't mean that the way it came out," Hank said.

"I don't think there's any way you meant something good." She turned away.

Hank looked at Jim. "I don't understand women."

Andrea nodded. "How true."

Grabbing his plate, Hank loaded it up. But tonight the food was tasteless. He pushed it around on his plate, eating little of it.

"You'll be happy to know that I made that peach cobbler," Jess said as she cleaned up. "But dessert has to wait until we put the tree up."

"Bribery, Jess?"

She looked at her husband. "Whatever it takes, honey."

Jim laughed. "Okay, we'll work fast, right, Hank?"

"But we want it done right," she warned them.

"Leave it to us."

Andrea met Hank's gaze. "We can help, too."

"Yeah," he said as he shared a superior look with Jim, "you girls can read us the directions."

TWO HOURS LATER they had the bottom half of the tree assembled. It filled up one corner of the living room and was more complicated to assemble than anyone had thought. But Andrea knew it'd be a stunner when it was done.

Hank had gone to get a stepladder so they could reach the heights.

Andrea sighed. "The top half will be harder to do."

"But we've done a good job so far," Jim told her, stepping back to assess their work.

"Yes, you have." Jessica wrapped her arms around him and gave him a kiss as a reward.

The gesture made Andrea feel lonely again. Watching the newlyweds, she had an urge to see Hank.

When he came back with the stepladder, she smiled at him, something she hadn't done since dinner.

Hank almost stumbled. Coming to a halt, he looked at her as if he needed to say something. But he didn't.

"Will that work, Hank?"

He nodded at her.

"Okay. On to the next level of branches." She handed him one.

"Jim, are you ready?" Hank said without looking at the couple with their arms around each other.

"Yeah, sure," Jim said, and kissed his wife.

"I think we girls are going to head to the kitchen and have a drink. We'll be back in a few minutes."

Hank watched as the two women walked out of the living room. "They're not going to eat dessert without us, are they?"

Chapter Seven

Andrea was making hot chocolate while Jessica whipped some fresh cream for the topping. "I'm having the greatest time tonight. I've always wanted to put up a Christmas tree."

"I know what you mean. Some of my fondest childhood memories have to do with Christmas. My dad was crazy about the holidays. He turned into a real Jimmy Stewart as soon as December rolled around." She got a wistful look. "I do miss him. And my mom."

Andrea couldn't empathize. She'd never had that kind of childhood or that kind of parent. Her mother was a cold gold digger and her father...well, she didn't know.

"Do you have to leave as soon as your month is up, Andrea?" Jessica asked, interrupting her thoughts.

"Why?"

Jessica smiled. "It's just that you're such fun to have around. I'll hate to see you go."

Andrea smiled back at the woman she'd come to think of as a friend. "I know what you mean. I'm enjoying it here, too."

"Just wait until you meet Mary Jo and Leslie. I know you'll like them."

"You know, when I decided to come here for a month, I figured I'd be bored in a couple of weeks. But now it seems such a short period of time."

Jessica brightened. "So you might stay a little longer? We could give you a job so you wouldn't still have to pay. Maybe Hank could use you to teach riding to the children."

"No, I can't stay." As much as she might like to, she had an appointment to get to. An important one.

"Oh."

At Jessica's dejected tone, she said. "Jessica, I'd love to stay, but I can't."

"Will your mother insist on your coming home?"

"No." Her mother didn't even know where she was, nor did she probably care. She was too busy with her husband.

Despair hit Andrea like a charging bull. Tonight was showing her just how alone she really was. She felt overwhelmed with the need to reach out to someone. To confide in someone. Maybe it was all the talk of childhood memories and fathers.

Jessica was the perfect shoulder to cry on. Andrea knew she could trust her.

"Remember when I arrived, I said I was going to visit someone?"

"Yes. I wondered if it was someone we knew. But you never said."

Andrea looked over her shoulder toward the doorway. "I can't talk about it here. What if the men come in?"

"Come upstairs." Jessica grabbed her hand and led her. When they reached Andrea's room, Andrea shut the door behind them and blurted it out. "I'm going to visit my father." The words sounded strange to her ears. *My father.*

"Your father?"

"Dan Peters, the man who sold Moonbeam to Hank, is my father."

Jessica's mouth fell open. "You know, all along I've been thinking you look like somebody. But I couldn't know who." She smiled broadly and grabbed Andrea's hands. "How marvelous! But why all the secrecy?"

"He doesn't know I'm here yet—and that's the way I want to keep it. Nor do I want anyone else to know yet."

Jessica reassured Andrea of her silence. "But I don't get it."

"It's complicated. You see…" Tears began to sting her eyes and she closed them tightly for a moment. "I haven't seen him—my father—for twenty-two years. He and my mother split when I was really little." She told Andrea how her mother had raised her in New York and her father had settled near Steamboat Springs, how her mother had remarried for money and had raised her with all the privileges anyone could ask for. Except the one she really wanted. Her father.

"Thinking about spending the holidays alone this year just felt depressing, so I looked my father up. I was so nervous, but I picked up the phone, dialed and suddenly we were talking. That's when he invited me out to Christmas."

"But why are you taking riding lessons when Dan can teach you?" Jessica asked softly.

"I wanted him to be proud of me." Andrea shrugged.

"I know it's silly. But I just have it in my head that he wouldn't want a spoiled city girl as a daughter." The tears that had threatened before now spilled down her cheeks, and she wiped them away. "I'm sorry."

"Don't be. I understand." Jessica patted her hand. "But you don't have to worry. I'm sure Dan will see the wonderful, accomplished, caring woman that we've come to know."

Andrea smiled through her tears. "Thanks." She sniffled. "Please promise me you won't say a word to anyone. I—"

A knock on her bedroom door interrupted her.

She put her finger to her lips and then got up to answer it, wiping her eyes. Straightening her back, she opened the door.

Hank and Jim stood in the hallway.

"What are you guys doing in there?" Jim asked.

"We…came up to get some tissues and just started talking," Jessica said hurriedly, coming to the doorway. "Have you finished the tree?"

"Yeah, we have. Want to come see it?" Jim asked, holding out his hand to his wife.

"Yes. Are you coming, Andrea?"

"Yes, of course." But as she stepped through the doorway, Hank took her arm, holding her back for just a minute.

"Are you upset about something?" he asked in a soft voice.

"No. Why would you say that?"

He searched her eyes, no doubt noticing their redness. But all he said was, "I just wondered."

She forced a smile. "Come on. I want to see the tree."

Hank nodded, but she caught the slight frown on his face. Apparently the man was more observant than she'd thought.

The women oohed and ahhed over the tree, praising the men's hard work.

"Now we'll do our part and dish up the dessert. Come to the kitchen," Jessica said.

She filled four bowls with warm cobbler and Andrea topped them with a scoop of vanilla ice cream.

"Man, this is great, honey," Jim said to his wife as he took a spoonful.

"Thanks. But you two did a terrific job on the tree."

"Yes, they really did." Andrea was keeping her head down as she ate. She hoped no one noticed.

"So what were you talking about upstairs?" Hank asked abruptly.

Andrea's gaze flew to Jessica, panic written on her face.

"Hey, it was girl talk. We don't ever share it with men, Hank."

Andrea was grateful for her confidante's quick thinking.

Judging from the narrow-eyed look Hank gave them, he wasn't convinced. "Sounds suspicious."

"Of course it does," Jessica said with a laugh. "But you'll just have to accept it, Hank. We're not going to tell you anything. Right, Andrea?"

Nodding, Andrea kept her head down and ate her dessert.

Apparently Hank wasn't satisfied. "But why—"

Jim cut him off with an outstretched palm. "Just let it go, Hank. Women can keep secrets. Trust me, they're like a vault with those things."

"ALL RIGHT, now tell me everything."

As soon as he shut their bedroom door behind him, Jim turned to his wife. "What were you talking about with Andrea?"

Jessica played coy. "The reason she came here." She started to undress, which always got Jim's attention. "I think that's the part I'm not supposed to tell you."

"What are you talking about?"

She just grinned and continued to undress. Jim crossed the room rapidly and caught her around her bare waist. "What are you talking about, Jess?"

"Do you promise not to tell Hank? Even if you think he should know?"

"I promise."

"Her father is Dan Peters, Hank's friend, the one he bought Moonbeam from."

Jim took a minute to digest the information. "So why is she hiding that fact?"

"She doesn't want her father to know she's taking riding lessons from Hank." Jessica told him Andrea's reasons and how she planned to spend Christmas with her father and the details of her parents' divorce. After all, though she'd promised Andrea, there were simply some secrets a wife couldn't keep from her husband.

"Did she tell her mother what she was doing for Christmas?"

"No. She and her mother don't really have any

Christmas traditions. She says her mother has gone to Switzerland with her husband to ski. For years Andrea had been wanting to meet her father, so she decided this was the perfect time. After she learned to ride, of course."

"Man, I'd like to see Hank's face when he learns all that."

Panic struck Jessica like a slap in the face. "But you're not going to tell him!"

"Relax, sweetheart, I won't."

"I promised Andrea I'd keep her secret. She can't find out that I told you, either, or—"

Jim reached out and pulled her close, cutting her off with a kiss. "Honey, we've got more important things to do now," he said with a suggestive look at the bed.

Jessica smiled.

"HANK, YOU HEARD Jessica. I can't tell you what we were talking about."

Ever since they set out riding that morning, Hank had been trying to get Andrea to tell him what she and Jess had talked about last night.

She determinedly changed the subject.

"Where are we riding today?" she asked.

He refused to answer. She wasn't answering *his* questions; he wouldn't answer hers.

When they dismounted for lunch, he tried one more time. "Do you still have nothing to say?"

"About what?"

"Andrea, this is ridiculous. You don't know Jessie well enough to share secrets with her."

"Yes, I do."

"Fine!"

They went in for lunch in silence.

Jessica looked up. "How was your morning?" she asked with a cheerful smile.

"Fine!" Hank snapped.

Andrea sent a look at Jessica.

"Hank, you're not still upset about last night, are you?" Jessica asked.

"Yeah!"

Andrea said nothing.

"You're being silly. Andrea doesn't have to tell you what we talked about!"

"I have a feeling it affects me. So I should know what you talked about."

"I think you're being ridiculous," Andrea said, then turned to Jessica. "Has he always been this way?"

"What? Stubborn? Absolutely."

"Jess, I've changed!"

"Sure you have, Hank. Just not enough."

"I've stopped fighting the dude-ranch idea."

"Only because Jim didn't give you an option."

"Yeah, but I cooperate now."

"You mean about Andrea's lessons? Yeah, you cooperated because, again, Jim didn't give you a choice."

"You didn't want to give me lessons?" Andrea asked.

"I—I was reluctant to teach you because…" He paused, trying to explain his decision. "I didn't want to have an assignment because it was my off time."

"I see," Andrea said.

"Andrea, I didn't know you! I thought you'd be a

stuck-up Yankee and not be willing to work as hard as you've worked."

"I think you misjudged me!"

"I know. That was before I met you."

"You didn't even like me when you met me!"

"Aw, now, you know that's not true, don't you?"

"I'm not sure!"

"I'll show you."

They started eating and felt silent. Andrea kept her gaze on him, wondering what he intended to do.

After lunch, when they went back out, Hank didn't talk about how he intended to convince her he was okay about the lessons. Until they reached the barn.

"Wait. Don't mount up yet."

Andrea stared at him. "Why not?"

"Because I'm going to show you that I'm okay with your lessons." And with that he pulled her into his arms and kissed her.

Ever since the night of their dinner in Steamboat Springs, Andrea had been thinking about Hank kissing her, but she hadn't expected him to do it now.

Hank wrapped his arms around her and she slipped hers around his neck. Feeling her surrender, Hank raised his head and reslanted his mouth across hers, taking it more fully. His tongue teased her teeth until she opened for him. He tasted like heaven.

Andrea had been kissed before, by some powerful, influential young men. But none of them set her on fire the way Hank did with one kiss.

He let her go only long enough to take a breath, then

claimed her mouth again. That momentary release was what she needed to regain her equilibrium.

What was she doing?

She pulled away. "Hank, we can't—"

But he insisted they could as his lips covered hers again. Then they both heard Jessica's voice calling for Andrea.

As if on fire, Andrea backed away from Hank. "I— I'd better go see what she wants." She rushed out of the barn.

Jessica was running toward her. "Come quick. You've got a phone call."

Andrea was confused. She had left a number with the maid back in New York in case of an emergency, but otherwise, she didn't think anyone had the number.

Jessica hurried her inside the house as a pickup pulled up beside the corral. She shut the door. "Wow, that was close."

"What? What just happened?"

"Your dad was coming to see Hank."

"My dad? He's out there?"

"Yes. Did you want to see him?"

"No! Not yet." Then, realizing how close she'd come to blowing her plan, she pulled Jessica close for a hug. "Thank you."

"I didn't think you wanted to see him yet. But Hank and Dan are pretty good friends."

"Really?"

"Yes. For the longest time Dan was alone. Then he and Hank found a friendship that's important to Hank. But after that, your dad married again."

"He did? I didn't know that."

"Actually, he should've married again sooner. He's only forty-six."

"Who did he marry?" Hearing this made Andrea think even more how much of a stranger her own father was. But she intended to change that.

If he'd have her.

"It's a really sweet story," Jessica said. "He fell for the kids first. You see, Barbara was a widow with two little boys. The oldest boy, Charlie, came out with his Boy Scout troop to see the Appaloosa horses. Charlie decided he wanted to be a cowboy. He begged his mother to take him back to Dan's ranch, so she called and asked. Your dad offered to give him lessons."

"That sounds very nice, but—"

"He gave both boys lessons. They were so small, but Charlie and Casey loved it. Afterward he'd offer to bring the boys in for a drink, assuming their mom would follow. But she always said they had to go home. One afternoon he told her his housekeeper already had a meal fixed for them, so she agreed to stay.

"The boys asked to come again, and their mother reprimanded them at once. But Dan gave them an open invitation. Then he also gave their mother an open invitation. The housekeeper reassured her, telling her that she hadn't seen Dan as happy as he was that day.

"They came out a lot more, and suddenly Dan noticed the mom more than he did the boys. But he thought he was too old for her. Barbara was only twenty-five and your dad was forty-five."

"I'm glad he's found a family, but why didn't he tell me?"

Jessica shrugged. "I suspect he was afraid you wouldn't come."

"Do you think I should go? I mean, Christmas is such a personal thing. Maybe my father doesn't want me there with his new family."

"I would think he's really looking forward to your coming. But I assumed you didn't want to meet him today."

"No, I have to prepare myself a bit more." Andrea looked over her shoulder at the window. "But I can look out, as long as he doesn't know I'm here." Before she got up, she turned to Jessica. "I really look like him?"

"You do. Especially around the eyes."

Jessica led her upstairs and she looked out one of the windows that offered a perfect view of the barn. "There he is," Jessica said.

Andrea stared at the man talking to Hank. He was tall, with sandy-brown hair under a white cowboy hat. Even under his sheepskin jacket she could see that he was broad and strong and fit. He threw his head back in laughter at something Hank said and she heard his deep voice.

Her father was everything she'd always dreamed he'd be.

Watching him, she remembered some things she'd forgotten about her daddy, like how he used to play with her, holding her way up above his head and spinning her. And she remembered his laugh.

Then Andrea glanced at his truck and saw two little boys. Charlie and Casey, no doubt, waiting for their daddy.

She pointed them out to Jessica.

"They're really cute, aren't they? And they're going to have a little brother soon."

"My father's going to have another child?" She couldn't believe it. She'd have a half brother. "When is he due?"

"I think they said in April."

"Oh, I want to stay here and get to know him!"

"Yeah, I'm sure."

"Oh, he's leaving!" Andrea cried.

"You can't go back out until he's gone. What are you going to tell Hank?"

She'd almost forgotten about Hank. "I'll tell him my mother called from Switzerland. He'll believe that."

"Yes, he will."

They came back down the stairs and Andrea turned to hug Jessica. "I want to thank you for telling me about his family, and for helping me hide from him for a little while longer."

"I'm glad I got there in time. When I saw him turn in the drive it was just luck that I could get you inside before he saw you."

"I know. I was a little confused because…uh, I mean…I wasn't sure…"

Jessica chuckled. "What are you trying to tell me?"

Andrea ducked her head, unwilling to meet Jessica's gaze. "Hank was kissing me."

Jessica shook her head. "I can't believe my brother. Andrea, don't count on him—"

Andrea cut her off. "I know. I'm not counting on anything. I've got to go. I'll see you this evening."

Andrea went back out to the barn and immediately mounted her horse.

"What happened to you?" Hank asked. "What did Jessie want?"

"I had a phone call. My mother."

"Oh, really?" Hank mounted his horse. "She doesn't want you to come home, does she?"

"No. She isn't at home. She's in Switzerland, skiing."

"Didn't she want you to go, too?"

She shook her head. "She's with her husband. She just called to see how I was doing."

"So what did you tell her?"

"I told her I was doing fine."

Hank grinned at her. "Did you tell her I kissed you?"

Her cheeks flamed. "Of course not!"

"Good."

He moved his horse next to hers and bent over to kiss her one more time. Then he lifted his head and rode forward, telling her to follow him.

After a little while, he waited for her to ride up beside him. "The man who came over is Dan Peters. He raises Appaloosas. Remember I told you he sold me Moonbeam."

"Too bad I didn't meet him." She was amazed at how easily the lie came out.

"Yeah, he couldn't wait because he was supposed to be home. His wife needs him for something—he just married her a few months ago."

"How nice for him." It seemed he'd found real love. Unlike her mother.

"I wanted to introduce you to Dan," Hank continued. "He's a great guy."

"Really? That would've been nice."

"Yeah, but you had to get a phone call just when he came over."

"I'm sorry."

"I guess we'll see him again before you leave."

"I guess so." She changed the subject. "So where are we riding today?"

"How about I take you to our mountain stream so we can be alone?"

That sounded perfect.

Chapter Eight

The afternoon sun glinted off the crystal waters as they approached the stream on horseback. Andrea had never seen a more beautiful sight. All around her the mountains rose to the blue sky, making her feel as if she could touch the puffy white clouds.

And beside her rode Hank. Sitting high on his horse, he pointed out all the places he'd ridden as a kid, how the snow would look when it finally hit. Clearly he loved the ranch.

"We'll dismount here and let the horses drink," he told her when they reached the stream.

Though Andrea was feeling strong, she let him hold her by the waist and lift her off Moonbeam, lowering her ever so slowly to her feet.

It was the perfect afternoon.

"I'd love to take a walk by the stream," she said. "Will the horses be okay?"

He looped their reins over a nearby branch and took her hand.

As they walked, she told him all about her job and

her life in the city. He told her about growing up on a ranch and his love for horses.

He pointed to a huge boulder alongside the stream. "You know, right here is where I got this scar." He pushed up his hat and pointed to a faint crescent of white skin at his hairline. "I was seven and I rode out here with my father, hell-bent on showing him how good a rider I was." He laughed. "Needless to say, I wasn't *that* good."

"I can see that." Andrea laughed. "You know, you haven't changed much."

He pretended to be affronted. "What are you trying to say?"

"You're still like that. You're still trying so hard to prove yourself. Only now it's to your sister and Jim." *And me,* she wanted to say, but didn't.

"I thought I'd already proved myself. Especially to you."

The look he gave her told Andrea exactly what he meant. And she agreed. Undoubtedly he was the best kisser.

"Or should I try again?"

She smiled at him. "By all means." And she stepped into his arms.

Hank took her lips with confidence. But it was the gentleness he showed that nearly undid her. His hands grazed over her back and then under her jacket, barely touching her, but leaving a trail of heat.

She knew then what it'd be like to make love to Hank.

Of course, that could never happen. But she could dream.

He pulled back and smiled at her, resting his forehead against hers. "How'd I do this time?"

"I'd give you a B plus."

"Next time I'll go for an A." He took her hand and they strolled back toward the horses.

They rode in a full-out gallop back to the ranch. Exhilarated, Andrea pulled up by the corral, then leaned over Moonbeam and stroked her. She could hardly believe she'd learned to ride this quickly—and she owed it all to Moonbeam. And Hank.

She turned to tell him that when someone called her name. Looking up, she saw one of the cowboys coming toward her. Slim, if she remembered correctly from the night of the singing auditions.

"Hey, Andrea. You're gettin' pretty good on that horse. Either the boss is a good teacher or you're just a good pupil." He smiled up at her and lent a hand as she dismounted.

Andrea was polite and made small talk, but all the while she kept looking for Hank.

WHO WAS SHE talking to?

Hank had ridden into the barn to unsaddle his horse, expecting Andrea to follow. When she hadn't, he noticed her by the corral with one of the cowboys.

Once Moonbeam moved out of the way, he saw it was Slim.

Damn. Couldn't Andrea see that cowboy was only interested in one thing?

He strode out to the corral, eating up the distance in

a few angry strides, and barked, "Any rider knows they've got to take care of their horse."

Andrea turned to him with a sharp look. "I was just saying hi to Slim."

"Yeah, well, your horse needs tending. Do it now." And he walked away.

He was unsaddling his horse when she led Moonbeam into the barn. He didn't look up.

"I don't appreciate being yelled at in front of other people."

She stood there, hands on her hips, all angry and confrontational.

"And I don't appreciate my animals being treated unfairly."

"This has nothing to do with Moonbeam and you know it. It's about Slim."

Apparently she was more astute than he gave her credit for. But he wouldn't give her the satisfaction she no doubt craved. "I don't care about Slim. Unsaddle your horse."

Then, to be sure he didn't take her in his arms again, he stormed out of the barn and up to the house.

He threw open the back door and strode into the kitchen.

"Hi, Hank."

"Hi, Mary Jo." Then he looked up and blinked. "Mary Jo? What are you doing here?" He hurried over to give her a hug. "Is Pete here?"

"Of course he is! He and Jim are bringing in our luggage."

"I'll go help them."

"That's nice of you, Hank, but Jim's already on it."

"What are you doing back so soon? I thought your honeymoon wasn't over till the end of November."

She smiled sheepishly. "I missed my kitchen."

"Well, Jessie took good care of it while you were gone."

"Also," said Mary Jo, "I wanted to be home to make Thanksgiving dinner." She looked at him quizzically. "Now what's got you so hot that you almost took off the kitchen door?"

Hank's mouth flattened. "Nothing." He turned to his sister-in-law. "Good to have you back. I've got to get cleaned up for dinner."

After Hank had gone to his room, Mary Jo asked, "Is he still mixed up with those women in Steamboat Springs?"

"Not exactly."

"What do you mean?"

"Wait until you see Andrea." Jessica had already told Mary Jo about their guest and Hank's new riding student.

"Does she have him wrapped around her finger?"

"No, I don't think so, but—"

The sound of the kitchen door slamming brought Jessica's explanation to a halt. Now it was Andrea's turn to storm into the house.

"I'm sorry," Andrea said when she saw the women in the kitchen. "I didn't mean to do that." She looked at the stranger and came to a halt. "Am I intruding? I can—"

"Not at all, Andrea. This is Mary Jo. She and Pete came back this afternoon."

Mary Jo held out her hand. "Welcome to the Lazy L, Andrea."

"Thank you. It's nice to meet you. Jessica has told me a lot about you." She smiled at Mary Jo.

"It's good to be back."

"Was your honeymoon fun?" Jessica asked.

"Oh, yes! I never thought Pete was romantic, but he definitely is. He spoiled me rotten. And tried to talk me out of coming back so soon."

"I know my brothers were difficult in the beginning," Jessica said, "but they really are good guys."

Andrea snickered.

Jessica stared at her. "Did he do anything bad today?"

Embarrassed that she'd let her feelings show, Andrea tried to backpedal. "No. Nothing."

Jessica wasn't deterred. "What happened?"

"Oh, he…just got irritated with me."

"Why?" both women chorused.

"I said hello to Slim."

"So why did Hank get mad?" Mary Jo asked.

Jessica leaned toward Mary Jo and stage whispered, "Jealousy."

Hank came back into the kitchen then, ignoring Andrea. "No sign of Pete?"

"Not yet."

"I guess I'll go find my brother since he hasn't come to me."

He walked out of the kitchen as quickly as he'd entered.

"You'll notice he didn't speak to me," Andrea said.

"Did you just wave or did you stop to talk to Slim?" Jessica asked.

"Well, I was passing him and he stopped me. We spoke a bit."

"Oh, so you actually talked to him?"

"I didn't want to be rude," Andrea said.

The two Ledbetter women looked at each other. Mary Jo nodded. "Definitely jealousy."

"DINNER IS READY."

Jessica ushered everyone into the dining room. The arrival of Mary Jo and Pete was a special occasion, and she had the table set with lovely linens.

The men stood talking when the women brought in platters of food and pitchers of drinks.

Mary Jo took the seat by Pete, and Jessica took the seat by Jim, which left only one seat for Andrea. By Hank.

She sat there, not wanting to cause a scene.

"This roast beef is delicious, Jessica," she said after she'd taken a bite.

Everyone agreed, except Hank. He said nothing. He was eating his meal with an intensity that left no room for conversation.

Pete looked at his brother. "You going into town tonight?"

"No, why?"

"You're eating like you've got plans for later."

"No, I'm just hungry. We rode a long way today."

Andrea raised her head. "We did? It didn't seem that far to me."

"That's probably because you enjoyed visiting with Slim so much!" Hank said through clenched teeth.

"I was just being polite!" Andrea returned.

"Damn it! It was unnecessary!"

"I disagree!"

"I don't care what you think. This is my home. I know how things work here."

"You've just been spoiled!"

Suddenly Hank pushed back from the table and stomped into the kitchen.

After a moment, Pete stood. "I'll just check on Hank."

Jessica put her hand on Jim's arm. "You're not going in there, are you?"

"No, I think I agree with Andrea."

Andrea perked up. "Good. I'm glad you agree with me, Jim."

"That doesn't mean I don't think you were torturing Hank." Jim leaned forward. "You had to know that would bother him."

Jessica stared at her husband. "How would she know that?"

"I think she was just being polite," Mary Jo said.

"This is not a sisterhood, ladies." Jim turned to Jessica "You agree with me, don't you?"

"I think it *is* a sisterhood, Jim. But you can join us."

"Maybe I'd better see how Hank is doing," he said as he stood.

"What? You're siding with Hank?" His wife was outraged.

"Let's just say it's a brotherhood." He walked off.

"Jessica, I'm sorry," Andrea said. "I didn't mean to… I didn't intend to argue with Hank. I'm just a little frustrated!" A tear slipped down Andrea's cheek despite her best efforts to hold it back.

"It's all right, Andrea," Mary Jo said. "Believe me, we know how these men are."

BY THE WEEKEND, the first snow of the season had fallen. But there was frost in the air inside, as well.

The men felt they had the right to stand their ground. The women felt they had the right to demand some understanding.

Andrea hadn't wanted an all-out war, but Jessica and Mary Jo assured her the battle wouldn't last. They had a plan.

On Sunday, the two women organized the tree decorating. To ensure that the men joined them, they planned a finger-food luncheon to be served in the living room.

After they arrived home from church, Mary Jo announced that they would be serving lunch in the living room in half an hour.

"Why are we eating in the living room?" Jim asked.

"Because we're decorating the big tree," Jessica explained. "We need to get it done and then evaluate what other decorations we need to buy." She began taking ingredients out of the refrigerator. "Will we see you then?"

"Uh, I guess so."

The three women had organized their menu the night before, and in half an hour a variety of finger foods was ready.

When they took the dishes into the living room, where

they'd previously set out the balls and special ornaments, the tree already twinkled with miniature white lights.

It was Andrea's plan that the guys got a piece of finger food for every ornament they placed on the tree. When the men came in a couple of minutes later, she explained the idea that she hoped would encourage them to participate in decorating the tree.

"I should've known. Another damn trap!" Hank exclaimed, and turned to leave.

"Hank, it was just a suggestion. If you want to eat and not decorate, that's fine, too." Andrea turned her back on him, so he wouldn't think she cared.

He came to a halt, his hands on his hips.

Pete took his brother's arm. "Come on back, Hank. What's a few ornaments? The food looks good."

"Yeah, come on, Hank. It's not that bad. So she talked to some other guy. It doesn't mean anything." Jim watched Hank's reaction.

"I think it did!"

"You've talked to some women, haven't you?"

Hank stared at his brother. "Yeah, but not lately."

"Well, I'm glad you stopped running into town all the time," Pete responded.

"The cheese bread is getting cold," Andrea said, awfully tired of this ridiculous argument. "It's much better when it's hot."

After a moment, Hank moved back toward the tree.

Jessica got Jim to put the star on top, and Mary Jo asked Pete to wrap the garland around the tree.

"Uh, sure, we will…won't we, Hank?"

"Yeah, I guess," Hank agreed reluctantly.

The two men found the garland and Hank used the stepladder after Jim got down. When he finished his part, Hank ambled back to the sofa and found something else to eat.

"These are really good," Hank said, holding up a fried broccoli bite in his hand.

"Andrea told me you'd like those," Jessica said. "I thought it was pretty nice of her to be concerned about your likes and dislikes after the way you've behaved."

Andrea stepped forward. "Jessica, don't—"

"I didn't ask her to do that!"

"No, it was just a casual observation," Jessica said calmly.

"I see." Hank turned to Andrea. "Thanks for these." Then he walked over to her and kissed her cheek.

Andrea, along with Jessica and Mary Jo, was left staring at him.

"What?" he asked.

Because Andrea remained speechless, Jessica spoke up. "I thought you were mad at Andrea. Aren't you?"

He grinned. "Not really. She just made me mad, talking to Slim like that."

Mary Jo looked at her husband. "Did you know he wasn't still mad at her?"

"Yeah. We talked him out of it."

"Well, you could've told me!"

"And divulge a secret? We men wouldn't think of it."

BY DINNERTIME the tree was finished.

Andrea had suggested they have their coffee in the living room so they could enjoy the festive atmosphere, and Hank was glad they did. The season's first Christmas music filled the air and the tree cast a warm glow on the unlit room—and on Andrea. She sat on the floor in front of the tree, admiring the ornaments. Hank admired her.

"It's beautiful," she said.

"Yes, it is, isn't it," Mary Jo said. "I'm so glad Pete and I got back in time to help with it."

They lounged in the comfortable room until everyone had finished their coffee. Then the couples went to bed, first Mary Jo and Pete, then Jim and Jessica.

"We've got, uh, some things to take care of upstairs," Jess told him. "Right, honey?"

Jim looked confused. But then he quickly replied, "Uh, yeah."

Hank knew his sister was orchestrating the evening, the same way she'd orchestrated the whole tree-decorating party. He couldn't say he wasn't grateful for leaving him alone with Andrea.

Now the rest was up to him.

Chapter Nine

Andrea looked away from the tree and realized she was alone with Hank.

"Where'd everyone go?" she asked.

"To bed. They said good-night, but you were too engrossed in those twinkling lights to hear."

She looked down at her watch. "Maybe I should turn in, too." She got up from the floor and walked behind the sofa he was sitting on.

Hank reached out and grabbed her arm as she went by. "Don't."

She looked down at him. "Excuse me?"

"You got to sleep late this morning, didn't you?" Hank asked.

"Yes, but I have to get up early tomorrow."

"You don't have to. I can tell your teacher to start class later in the morning." He grinned.

Andrea hesitated.

"Come on. Sit with me. We can finish listening to the Christmas carols. I promise I'll behave."

Now he'd gone and done it, Hank thought. Why did he have to promise her? He had a romantic setting, with soft lights and soft music, and the most beautiful woman—and he'd promised to be good!

Andrea came around and sat beside him.

They sat quietly for a while, then Hank asked, "Are you pleased with the first Christmas tree you've ever trimmed?"

"More than pleased. I'd always wanted a tree-trimming party. Now I'll make sure I have one every year."

Hank didn't want to think about Andrea returning to New York, though their time together was rapidly coming to an end. He wanted to make the most of what they had left.

Leaning toward her, he pulled her closer to him on the sofa and put his arm around her. Before she could utter a protest, he kissed it from her lips.

She tasted of raspberry-flavored coffee, candy cane and chocolate. An unbeatable combination.

He took another small taste, then another, until Andrea sighed under his lips.

It was all the invitation he needed. He pulled her against him, her breasts moving against his chest with each breath she took, and gave her the openmouthed kiss he'd thought about all night.

Andrea gave him the access he demanded.

His promise be damned. He brought his hand around and slipped it under her sweater, feeling her shiver when his fingers touched her sensitive flesh. And still she kissed him. Bolder now, he moved his hand upward and cupped her breast. The action was enough to bring him to the point of no return. What was it about this woman that affected him so?

Andrea gasped when he worried her nipple between his forefinger and thumb. She pulled back and took his hand away.

He'd gone too far.

"Hank, I don't think we should be doing this."

"Why? Don't you like it?"

She shook her head. "It's…"

"Enjoyable?"

Instead of answering, she stood up. "I need to get some sleep."

He stopped her again. "I have a question for you."

"What?"

"Are you a virgin?"

She stared at him, her mouth agape. Then she caught herself and put her hands on her hips, suddenly indignant. "That's none of your business."

"I think it is. If you aren't a virgin, then there isn't any reason for you to go to your room alone."

Her eyes glittered in the tree light. "I *am* going to my room alone—so I can get some sleep!"

"I think we'd sleep a lot better together." He flashed her a sexy grin.

"No chance." Then she pulled from his grip and started up the stairs.

Halfway up, she stopped and turned back to him. "Remember, you promised we could go for an overnight trip once Pete and Mary Jo returned."

Hank rubbed his neck. Another of his many promises.

"I guess I did promise, didn't I? Then we'd better do that."

"Thanks, Hank." She smiled at him, then walked out of his line of sight. He heard her door shut behind her.

Hank sat there with his head in his hands. The night certainly hadn't gone the way he'd planned.

Blowing out a breath, he got up, turned off the tree lights and the CD player. No need for them now. Then he went into the kitchen with the two coffee cups.

Pete found him there a while later.

"What are you doing up?" Hank asked.

"Waiting on my wife. She needs a drink of water."

"We didn't think of putting glasses up there. Sorry, Pete. But I think they did a good job on the carpentry." When Pete married Mary Jo, and Jessie married Jim, they had some interior remodeling done.

"I meant to thank you. With MJ's room and Jessie's room, we both got much larger bedrooms."

"Yeah, we did." Hank thought about his siblings with their spouses. "If it weren't for the Labs, I might get real lonely."

Pete chuckled. "Are they in your room at night?"

"Yeah. They sleep on a couple of carpet pieces stacked up. They keep me company." He whistled for the two dogs and they came running. "Gotta let them out for the last time tonight."

"Well, I'd better get this water up to MJ." He turned to leave, then stopped. "By the way, I like Andrea a lot. She fits right in, doesn't she?"

"Yeah, almost like she belongs here."

Pete clapped his brother on the back. "Well, I know how you can fix that!" Pete grinned at him.

"Good night," Hank said, not a trace of a smile on his face.

THE NEXT MORNING when Andrea came down, she found Mary Jo back in the kitchen preparing breakfast. Andrea pitched in, setting the table and cooking the bacon while Mary Jo made scrambled eggs and sausage. When the oven buzzer went off, she took out beautifully browned biscuits.

"You're such a good help, Andrea," Mary Jo said. "Thank you."

"I just do the easy parts. If I made biscuits, everyone would probably break a tooth!"

One by one the Ledbetters came in and sat down to eat.

"Will you two be coming in for lunch?" Mary Jo asked Hank and Andrea.

Hank stopped eating long enough to answer. "I think this might be a good day for us to ride with the cowboys, Andi, if you think you can make it."

"Do I have a nickname now?" Andrea smiled. "Yes, I think I can, and if I can't, I can unsaddle Moonbeam by myself."

"In that case, then, Mary Jo, we'd like a bagged lunch."

"No problem."

Andrea felt special being allowed to ride with the cowboys that day. She went out and got Moonbeam from her pasture, putting the bridle on her and leading her to the barn. There she saddled the mare by herself.

She was the first one mounted. Having stored her

sandwich in her saddlebag, along with an apple, she relaxed as the men saddled their horses.

"Seems like my little brother did a good job teaching you to ride, Andrea," Pete said.

"Yes, he did. I hope I can ride all day with you."

"Has he put a limit on your riding?"

"No, I determine when I'm too tired to ride. But we've put in full days…most of the time."

Hank pulled up his horse beside her, but didn't say anything.

"Why didn't you tell your brother our routine?" she asked him.

"I didn't have to. Miss Jacobs, you did me proud."

BY ABOUT FOUR O'CLOCK that afternoon, Andrea knew she'd hit her limit. They'd got out of the saddle for lunch. She'd enjoyed that time, spent together in the shade of a tree. But when she got back in the saddle, she'd found it difficult. Hank had hung around when they mounted. She'd known he was waiting to see if she could get back in the saddle.

She had, but she was fading fast.

She was near Jim when his cell phone went off.

"They are?" he said.

He motioned the other two closer.

Andrea was hoping they needed to go back to the house.

"We'll be right there." Jim added before he hung up.

"Granddad and Leslie are home. The girls want us to come in early. I'll tell Slim to carry on."

Hank turned to Andrea. "You'll like Granddad, and Leslie is wonderful."

"I'm just grateful for a reason to go in early," she muttered under her breath.

"You did well today. But I figured you were ready for an early end to it. I was about to suggest it."

The four of them were soon riding toward the house at a lope. Thanks to Hank's teaching, the pace relaxed her. When they reached the barn, Andrea didn't ask for help. She unsaddled Moonbeam and rubbed her down before she turned her out into the pasture.

Hank said, "Good job, Andi. I was going to help you, but you were too quick."

"Thanks. But I'm coming to enjoy unsaddling Moonbeam."

"And you can ride like that?"

An older gentlemen came out of the shadows. "You must be Andrea. And Hank's right. You did a fine job."

Hank hastily said, "Granddad, this is Andrea. Andrea, this is my grandfather, Cliff Ledbetter."

He had graying hair, but a fit body from a lifetime of outdoor work. Looking at him, Andrea knew exactly what Hank would look like in forty years. "Hello, Mr. Ledbetter. I'm delighted to meet you."

"Me, too. You from around here?"

"No, sir, I'm from New York."

"Well, for a New Yorker, you ride well."

Andrea smiled. "Thanks, sir. Hank taught me."

"Good job, boy." Cliff clapped his grandson on the back.

"She's a good student," Hank replied.

They all went to the kitchen where they found Leslie and made the introductions.

"Let's move to the dining room where we can all sit down," Jessica said. Andrea quickly took another chair, hoping not to move for a while.

"How did you manage such a long ride, Andrea?" Mary Jo asked.

"It was okay, but I was pretty tired and ready to come in."

"I bet you were. I can ride, but not as long as you," Mary Jo said.

"I've gotten better. I can take care of Moonbeam before I come to the house. The first couple of days Hank had to carry me."

"You must've pushed her hard, boy. You should've been a bit more gentle," Cliff said.

Hank had nothing to say to that.

Mary Jo and Leslie brought out pieces of carrot cake for everyone. Then they went back in for coffee. Andrea started to get up to help them serve, but she found her legs weren't ready. She apologized.

Leslie laughed. "You're a guest, young lady. We don't expect you to help out."

"I'm afraid she's been helping out since she got here, Leslie." Jessica turned to Andrea. "And I'm not sure we would've made it without her."

"That was kind of you," Leslie said.

The men were talking about how things had gone on the ranch in the past few weeks. Hank told Cliff about the thieving ranch hands he had to let go, and Jim assured him they still had evening entertainment.

"Well, you've handled everything very nicely," Cliff said. "See, Leslie? You were worried about them for no reason. We didn't need to come back at all."

Leslie rolled her eyes, letting them all know who had been worried.

Andrea was feeling a little closer to normal by the time she finished her cake and coffee. She decided to help gather the dishes and then go upstairs and take a little nap.

Mary Jo joined her in the kitchen, "You don't have to help, Andrea. I can do it."

"I don't mind." She loaded the dishwasher with the cups and plates. "Is something wrong with Jessica?"

"Why do you ask?"

"She's eating very slowly and didn't even notice that we started clearing the table."

"I don't know. She was having trouble with several things today. She says she's feeling fine, but I'm watching her."

"If I can do anything, just let me know."

After they finished cleaning up, Andrea went upstairs. She lay on the bed with a sigh of contentment. In no time her eyes closed.

ON THANKSGIVING, when Andrea came down for dinner, the dining-room table was festively decorated and set for eight. She went into the kitchen to see if there was anything she could do. The smell of roasted turkey was heavenly.

"No, thanks, Andrea. We've got it all taken care of," Mary Jo said.

"How's Jessica?" She noticed she wasn't downstairs.

"She took a nap. Jim went up to wake her."

They both heard footsteps coming down the stairs.

When Jessica came in the kitchen, both Mary Jo and Andrea greeted her warmly.

"How are you feeling?" Mary Jo asked.

"I just feel tired. Like I'm running in water."

"Maybe you're coming down with the flu. Sometimes you feel the worst before you find out what's wrong."

"I don't know, Andrea. It will probably go away quickly. I can't imagine feeling this way for a week."

"Go sit down, Jessica. We're almost ready for dinner. Cliff and Leslie should be here any moment."

"I'm so glad they came back for the holiday," Jessica said.

"Cliff probably also wants to talk to Hank about a sale he heard about. He thinks Hank should add a few horses."

Andrea was pleased for Hank's sake. "I'm sure he'll be excited about that."

Within a few minutes, they were sitting around the table, enjoying a turkey dinner with all the trimmings.

Hank whispered to Andrea, "Did you hear that Granddad wants me to buy a few more horses?"

"Yes, that sounds great. When are they having the sale?"

"On Saturday. Do you want to go?"

"Do you think I would be of any help?"

"Sure. It would be like a test to see if you've learned anything."

"I think I have, but we'll see. Where is it?"

"Just west of Denver. A couple of hours away."

"I'd love to go."

Jessica overheard them. "Where are you going?" she asked.

"Hank says I can go to the horse sale and show him I listened to all his talk about horses. Kind of like a test."

Jess chuckled. "That'll be great."

"Did you really listen to him?" Cliff asked.

"Every word. He's taught me a lot about horses."

"Good. I'm glad you're learning." Cliff chewed for a moment, then asked, "Do you have any relatives here?"

"Why do you ask?" Andrea tried to keep her alerted nerves from showing.

"You just look familiar."

"I'm afraid not," she said with a forced smile.

Before Cliff could question her further, the phone rang. Cliff got up to answer it.

"That was my niece in Kansas City," he explained when he returned. "Do you remember Aunt Jennifer?" He looked at his three grandchildren.

Pete finally said, "I think they came for Christmas one year when I was a kid."

"Why did she call?" Jessica asked.

"Her mother, Marty, died this morning. We're going to have to go to the funeral."

"In Kansas City?"

"Yeah. I know it's a long way, but I think the three of you should go with me and Leslie," Cliff said. "It's an afternoon funeral. We can leave early that morning and come back that evening."

"When's the funeral?" Jessica asked.

"Saturday."

Andrea didn't have to look at Hank to feel his disappointment. He'd miss the horse sale.

It had been his chance to prove himself to his grandfather.

And their chance to be alone.

SATURDAY MORNING Andrea got up when it was still dark. She'd been looking forward to the horse sale, but it wouldn't be the same going with Jim, who was Cliff's designee. She dressed in her cowboy shirt, jeans and boots, but when she opened her door to go downstairs, she found Jim about to knock.

"Andrea, can you come in and help Jessica? She's been throwing up and I need to get Mary Jo."

"Of course." Andrea went into the bedroom and found Jessica sitting on the bathroom floor, holding a towel to her mouth.

"Jessica, are you all right?"

"Not really. I must have the flu. I can't go to the funeral."

"No, of course not. I'm sure your grandfather will understand."

"I hope so."

As if on cue, Cliff and Jim came in. Jim went right to her side. "Honey, I've got to go to the horse sale. Hank's counting on me to bring home a few horses."

"I'll be fine," Jess said. "I'll try to sleep."

"Cliff, you and Leslie and the guys had better get started to the airport," Jim said. "Andrea and I will leave in another hour or two."

Once Jessica was settled in her bed, Andrea left to get ready. As she walked down the hall, a door opened and she was pulled into a bedroom.

Strong arms wrapped around her and a familiar voice whispered, "Good morning."

She looked up at Hank and smiled. "It would have been a better morning if I was going to the horse sale with you."

"I know. I was looking forward to it, too. But Grand-dad really wants us to go to the funeral. He doesn't ask for much."

She nodded, knowing he was right.

"Just remember what I taught you," he told her. "I'm trusting you to do me proud."

"I will, Hank."

Before he let her go, he added, "There's one more thing to remember…"

He grabbed her upper arms in his strong hands and took her mouth in a kiss she'd never forget.

Chapter Ten

The horse sale was in full swing, buyers from all over the West converging on the Denver fairgrounds. Andrea felt the excitement to her bones, even though she was vastly out of her element.

She was used to crowds—she'd ridden the subway at rush hour. But she wasn't accustomed to seeing this many men in cowboy hats and boots.

One cowboy in particular popped into her mind. Too bad he wasn't here. She touched her lips. But she'd certainly remember his kiss.

Amid the noise she heard Jim's cell phone ring. He'd been calling every half hour to check with Mary Jo about his wife's condition, and judging from his half of the conversation, she was awake now.

"She's going to the doctor," Jim told her when he'd ended the call. "She did manage to eat some breakfast, but I'll feel better once the doc looks at her."

Jim went back to business, taking Andrea to look at the horses. They were grouped in several corrals all around the grounds.

Andrea tried to remember everything Hank had told

her about horses. She had made some notes last night and gotten Hank to read them over.

As they moved from one corral to another, Andrea realized how much Hank had taught her. She offered her opinions and was pleased when Jim concurred. They soon had a list of horses they believed filled the needs of the Lazy L.

As they took their seats under the tent for the auction, excitement buzzed in Andrea. She watched Jim handle the paddle once the bidding started, and she agreed with his moves. One horse in particular interested her. The bay mare's disposition was so gentle, she could easily see the horse being used for children.

The mare was the last of the four horses they bought, and Andrea was thrilled.

Jim loaded the new horses into the trailer and they started back. Once again he called the ranch. Apparently Jessica answered. "How are you?" Jim asked. "Did you see the doctor?"

Andrea waited anxiously for the call to end, and when it did, Jim told Andrea the news.

"She's okay, nothing serious. Said she'd tell me more when I was home—that'll be a couple of hours."

He drove silently for a few minutes, then said, "I meant to tell you how well you did today, Andrea."

"Thanks. I missed Hank, but it was like he was there. I kept hearing him tell me things in my head." And she felt his lips on hers, she added silently.

Jim grinned. "I'll be sure to tell him."

When at last they started down the mountain into

Steamboat Springs, Andrea sighed. "It's good to come home."

"You're so right. I'm glad you think of our home as your home."

Something about the way Jim said it sent a chill up her arms. "Jessica told you, didn't she."

"I'm afraid so. But she made me promise not to say anything to anyone else," he hurriedly added.

"Good." Strangely enough, she wasn't upset. She could understand a wife's need to confide in her husband and knew the secret would go no further.

"Do you plan to tell Hank?"

She shook her head. "Not right away. I want to get to know my father first."

"Yeah, I can understand that. Dan's a great guy."

"Thank you."

"No problem. But he's Hank's best friend."

She recalled how close she'd come to being outed when Dan had visited the Lazy L. Still, she needed to meet her father on her own terms. "I think I need time with my father without interruptions. It's been a long time—" She stopped herself. "It's been a lifetime, actually."

"I know. I just think you've formed a…friendship with Hank that could be important."

She hoped so.

When they pulled into the ranch, tired after a long day, Andrea knew they still had a lot of work to do. The horses had to be unloaded and checked out.

"What pasture do we put them in?"

"You don't have to do that, Andrea. You must be exhausted."

"Hank taught me more than just riding a horse. You don't leave a job half done. Now, what pasture?"

"The one we keep our rides in. Hank will want to look at them in the morning."

"Okay. Do we take their bridles off?"

"Yeah. Just put them in the barn."

They got the first two horses out and settled in the pasture and were on their way back to the truck when Mary Jo and Jessica came outside. Andrea saw Jessica fly into Jim's arms, and for the umpteenth time today she missed Hank.

She took both the remaining horses to the pasture and released them. When she came back to the barn, Jim thanked her.

"I'll take care of the trailer, Jess. Go in and get warm." He turned to Mary Jo. "You, too. And thanks for taking care of Jess today."

"Not a problem."

As Andrea walked alongside him back to the truck to get her things, he asked her, "Do they both seem happy to you? But who's happy to be sick?"

She shrugged. They'd find out soon enough.

JIM AND ANDREA were on dessert when Jessica asked to have a moment alone with her husband. Andrea left.

"Now are you going to tell me what the doctor said?" he asked.

"He said I was perfectly healthy."

"But did he figure out why you were throwing up?"

"Absolutely. He said it was normal during the first three months of a pregnancy."

"What?" Jim sat there, still, as the words settled in. Then he burst into a broad grin, picking her up and twirling her around. "That's great! Are you feeling all right now? You're not sick?"

"Not as long as you don't spin me around again," she said with a laugh.

"But will you be sick every morning?"

"I hope not. I'm supposed to eat soda crackers before I even get out of bed."

"That'll work?"

"He said to try it…and not get up until I feel good."

"That's a deal. We can cut back on your job and start you about ten every day."

"There's no need for me to retire! I just may have to take a nap every once in a while."

"Of course!"

ANDREA OPENED the kitchen door. "Did you tell him?"

"Yes!" Jessica said with a broad grin.

Jim blinked at Andrea. "You knew?"

Andrea nodded. "Mary Jo told me in the living room." She ran to Jessica and hugged her. "Congratulations! I'm so happy for both of you."

The scene would've been repeated when the rest of the family returned, but their flight was delayed by storms. Andrea turned on the weather channel and watched the rain pummeling Kansas City.

Then Pete called from the plane to say they'd finally taken off.

Once they were reassured that everything was fine, they went to bed. But Andrea couldn't sleep. She had so much on her mind. Her father. The new horses. Returning to New York.

And the thoughts all had one thing in common. Hank.

HANK DRAGGED HIMSELF in for breakfast the next morning. They'd finally gotten home after two in the morning, and seven o'clock came way too early.

He found everyone up except Jessica. But that was understandable.

Jim had told him the news last night when he'd met up with Hank in the kitchen about three. Jim couldn't sleep, but Hank guessed being told you were about to become a father would do that to a man.

They were all chattering when Pete suddenly asked, "Where's Jessie? Is she sick again?"

"No," Jim said. "The doctor told her to sleep in."

"That's all he could do for her feeling sick to her stomach?"

Jim shrugged. "Happens to some women when they're pregnant."

"Jess's pregnant?"

Jim beamed at Pete. "Yeah. Isn't it great?"

"You've got to tell Granddad. He'll be over the moon!"

Hank said, "Yeah, he's always telling us we're waiting too long."

"Yeah, but I'm thirty-one," Jim said. "I couldn't wait any longer, not once I saw Jess. Of course, I couldn't get her to talk to me at first. She was too busy yelling at you two." Jim grinned at Pete and Hank.

"Yeah, good thing we learned our lessons," Hank said. Then, after a pause, "So how did the horse sale go?"

"We looked at all the horses and then both of us, me and Andrea, graded them. And we came up with the perfect horses for us. Andrea was great."

Hank looked at Andrea. "Good job, Andi."

"Thank you. I just studied my notes."

"I can't wait to see the horses."

Their grandfather came in just then. "You all getting a late start?"

"Well, we're catching up on the news, Granddad. You might want to sit down with a cup of coffee," Pete said.

Mary Jo set a mug down in front of him.

"Thanks, Mary Jo. Is Jessie sleeping in this morning? I thought you said she was well."

"She's as well as any pregnant lady," Jim announced.

Cliff went off like a firecracker. "Mercy! That's wonderful!"

"But she doesn't want to be pampered too much. She's already warned me about that. She wants to continue doing her job."

"But can she ride a horse?"

"Yeah, but I'm not sure that's a good idea."

Andrea spoke up. "While I'm here I can help Hank, if he doesn't mind."

"That'd be fine with me." Hank reached for her hand and looked at his grandfather. "Jim tells me they did a good job at the horse sale."

"Great, though I think you might need a couple more horses. Does Dan have any he can sell you?"

"I thought I'd call him after I see these horses they bought yesterday."

"Good, good! Seems things are really going well."

"I think you're right, Cliff," Jim said. "By Christmas next year, we'll have a newborn. I can't wait!"

"Hey, we may join you."

Hank looked up to see who was talking. Pete was beaming at them.

"Whoa! What would we do if Mary Jo can't work?" Cliff protested. "Who would be our cook?"

"Wait a minute! It's okay for Jessie to be pregnant, but no one else?" Pete looked around the table. "I don't think I like the sound of that."

"Now, boy, don't be ridiculous. I just thought—"

"I think that's kind of hard for me and Mary Jo. We have to schedule our baby for your convenience?"

"No, I didn't mean that. I wasn't thinking about… You've only been married a month. I didn't think you'd be in such a hurry for… I mean, it didn't seem… Uh, could someone help me out here?"

Hank stood up. "I hope everyone married has kids as soon as they want. Then there won't be any pressure on me. I'm going to see the horses. Andi, you want to come out with me?"

"Yes, I do." They ran for the door.

"GRANDDAD'S A CRAZY MAN this morning, isn't he?" Hank asked on the way to the barn, sure Andi would agree with him.

She didn't respond.

He stopped and looked at her. He knew what her silence meant. "What did I say?"

"I don't think he's crazy."

"You don't?"

"No. I can understand his concerns. You've started this wonderful ranch and he's afraid it'll crash and burn."

"Surely two women pregnant wouldn't ruin everything. They'll work something out. But it won't affect me. I'm not married!"

He noticed her scowl.

"Hank, don't you ever want to be a father?"

This was one line of questioning he didn't need today. Not on a few hours' sleep. Trying to avoid it, he asked instead, "Why are we talking about this when we've got horses to look at?" He started walking again.

Andrea sighed, but went along, even picked up the pace to the pasture. "I need to tell you that one of the horses is pregnant."

"Damn! You bought a pregnant horse? I didn't ask for a pregnant horse!"

"You asked us to buy the best horses we could find."

"How did you know she was pregnant?"

"She seemed a little large and I asked Jim. He asked one of the cowboys running the sale. The guy said she was, but they weren't advertising it. Said he thought she was the buy of the sale. Her last foal had been a colt and he'd done real well."

"Andi, you can't be sucked in like that. The owners

tell those cowboys what to say. You've probably wasted money. Damn, I should've gone with you. It was asking too much to let a beginner go to the sale!"

"Well, excuse me!" She whirled and took a step back to the house, but Hank grabbed her arm.

"Wait, don't get upset. We asked too much of you. I'll find a way to get rid of her."

"If you do that, I'll never speak to you again!"

She wrenched her arm out of his hold and ran back to the house.

"Damn. I can't win this morning!"

He turned to stare out at the pasture where Jim said they'd put the horses.

He heard Jim asking Andrea where she was going. Hank rolled his eyes. Great. Jim would think he was disrespecting his opinion, too.

He waited until Jim reached his side.

"I hear you're getting rid of one of the horses we bought."

"That's the plan. We don't need any pregnant horses to go with the pregnant wives around here."

Jim looked offended. And rightly so, Hank realized. "Sorry, Jim. I didn't mean that the way it sounded. It's just—"

Jim interrupted him. "Don't you think you should look at this horse? She's a fine animal."

"Sure, I'll look at her. Then I'll find someone to take her, even at a loss."

"Okay, just as long as you look at her first. We both thought she was the best buy."

"Come on, Jim, you know they always have people

working these sales who'll tell you anything you want to hear."

"But this cowboy used to work for me. I told him we had a job open if he was interested."

"And he told you the stuff about this horse and about how he'd be perfect for the Lazy L?"

"Actually he did. He was surprised by our question. He said no one had noticed her pregnancy, but Andrea did."

Hank snickered. That was the problem, wasn't it. Andrea had babies on her mind.

That was one trap he'd have to avoid. Which meant avoiding her until she left.

Chapter Eleven

Andrea was furious! No matter what happened today, she would not go back outside with Hank.

"Andrea? Is everything all right?" Mary Jo asked when she stormed into the kitchen.

"Nothing's all right. Not as long as Hank Ledbetter is on this ranch."

Mary Jo poured two cups of coffee and took them to the table. "Come on and sit down with me. Spill everything."

Andrea did. She told her how Hank had given her a lecture about the pregnant horse.

"But you got two for the price of one," Mary Jo said. "Isn't that good?"

"You would think so! But he's decided he'll get rid of that horse without even looking at her. He told me *he* wouldn't have made that mistake!"

"So what are you going to do?"

"Stay out of his way. I thought maybe I could help you today."

"Sure. I was going to get ready for our first onslaught of guests. How are you at menu planning?"

HANK HATED to admit he was wrong. But in this case, he was.

After he had checked out the pregnant mare with Jim looking on, he'd had to agree with Andrea and Jim. She was a fine animal and a good buy.

Now he was leaning against the fence and thinking that maybe he'd been too harsh in his words to Andrea.

But he didn't want to admit it.

Jim ambled over. "What are you doing?"

"Waiting for Andrea to come back out for her riding lesson."

"Are you sure she's coming?"

"Of course. She just has to get over her anger."

"Yeah. But in my experience, when you've made a mistake, you need to apologize. An angry woman can hold grudges against you."

Hank said nothing.

"Well, are you going to apologize to her?"

Andi was blowing this out of proportion. "When she comes out, I will. In the meantime, I've got to work on the tack. There are some repairs I need to make."

"Okay. I'm going to go check out the cabins to see if there's anything to fix in them."

"If you run into Andi, tell her I'm waiting for her."

He'd apologize if he had to. But he wasn't chasing her down to do it.

ANDREA WAS KNEE-DEEP in recipes when Jim came into the kitchen.

"I just talked to Hank. He said he's waiting for you to come out for your lesson, Andrea."

"Not right now," she told him, holding her anger in check. She wouldn't take it out on Jim; he'd been so kind to her. Unlike Hank. "I'm helping Mary Jo work out a menu for the first week of guests."

"They'll be here before you know it."

Andrea didn't have much time left here. It saddened her, but then again, at least she'd be rid of Hank.

"I'm going to check the cabins to see what needs to be done before then, too," he said.

Jessica, who'd come down a few minutes earlier, wanted to go with him.

"Not before you eat some breakfast," Jim said.

"But I've already lost two hours!"

Andrea added a plea for reason. "You don't want to get run-down, Jessica. You need to stay strong for your baby."

"Then can you wait until I eat, Jim?" Jessica asked.

"Sure, if Mary Jo can bring me a cup of coffee," he said with a smile.

"I'll make a fresh pot," Mary Jo said. "Leslie's on her way."

When Leslie arrived, Jim got up and pulled up an extra chair for her.

"I thought I'd see what else needs to be done," the older woman said. "I can't believe we open at the end of next week."

"Do you want to check some of the bingo prizes?" Jessica asked her.

"Sure, I'll see what we've got. Maybe we won't have to shop for a couple of weeks."

"I'm available for shopping, Leslie, if you want company," Andrea offered. Anything to stay away from the stables.

"Is Hank too busy for riding lessons today?"

"Yes." Amazingly, the lie rolled easily off her tongue.

"Well, you could be taking the day off to relax, then."

"No. Too boring."

"In that case," Leslie said, rising to her feet, "let's all get to work."

By the time their respective chores were done, it was lunchtime. Andrea noticed six place settings at the kitchen table, even though she wasn't sure Hank would turn up for lunch.

He came in after they'd all sat down.

"Hi, Hank. Have a seat," Mary Jo said.

Hank stared at the seating. Andrea had taken the seat farthest from the empty one. He took the chair with a muttered thanks.

Leslie said brightly, "Have you had a good morning?"

"Not really. Somewhere I lost my student."

Leslie glanced at Andrea. Then back at Hank. "Oh?"

"Yeah. She didn't bother to show up for her lesson. I worked on tack all morning."

Silence descended on the kitchen, till Jim finally said, "Maybe you should tell Andrea about the horses we bought on Saturday."

"Yeah. You made some good choices, Jim."

"I didn't make the choices by myself, Hank," Jim said pointedly.

Andrea had had enough. She stood up abruptly, pushing her chair back. "I'll start the dishes." Picking up her plate and glass, she walked toward the kitchen. But not before she noticed Hank.

He just kept on eating.

JIM WALKED OUT to the barn with Hank.

"You didn't exactly apologize to Andrea at lunch."

"Nope."

"Why not? You know you said the wrong things to her earlier."

"I'm the one in charge of the horses. I can decide what horse goes or stays."

"Andrea knows that, Hank." Jim took off his hat and ran a hand through his hair. "You know, on the trip, she kept talking about how much she missed you. And then you go and insult her."

"You weren't there, Jim! Just because she got mad doesn't mean it was my fault."

"Okay, but what are you going to do about her riding lessons?"

"I'm here when she shows up. I'm not dragging her out by her hair!"

"And if she doesn't come out?"

"Then she's not getting her money's worth."

"Suit yourself." Jim turned and walked back to the house.

When he went to the kitchen, he discovered Andrea getting ready to drive into Steamboat Springs with Leslie to buy more bingo prizes. "Andrea, aren't you going to ride today?"

"No, I don't think so. Mary Jo said she might ride with me tomorrow."

"Okay. But Hank—"

"Hank has nothing to do with it!"

Jim drew a deep breath, as if he was about to say something, then he simply left the room.

Leslie said, "Are you sure you want to go with me? I can do it by myself."

Andrea smiled. "I'm sure. I'm not going to ride with Hank, so this is the perfect thing for me to do."

"Okay, then, let's head for the stores!" Leslie said with a grin.

They got in Leslie's car and drove into town. They went through the various stores that had possible prizes. They really enjoyed their shopping, and they really enjoyed each other's company.

"Leslie, I wish you and Cliff had come back earlier," Andrea said. "You're so much fun."

"You're the funny one. I think you should start a career as a stand-up comedian."

"I'd starve to death doing that for money."

"True. You don't have enough fat on you to last long."

"I'll take that as a compliment, Leslie."

"Good. Now we've got to get home or we'll miss dinner."

On the drive back to the house, they were slowed down by a snowstorm. It was well past dinnertime when they arrived.

"I hope they've saved us some dinner," Leslie said.

When they got inside, brushing off the snow, Mary Jo came out of the kitchen. "Thank goodness you're here! We've been worried about you two."

"Did you save us any dinner?" Leslie asked.

"Yes, Cliff made sure I did."

"I'll just tell the others that you two are back."

They'd just started eating when Cliff came in to greet his wife. Then he chastised her about driving in the snow.

"She did a great job of driving, Cliff." Andrea thought she should support Leslie.

"I don't like her taking chances."

"Dear, we were shopping! We didn't notice there was so much snow until we were halfway home."

Jim and Jessica joined them to chat, pulling up chairs.

"Did you get good prizes?" Jessica asked.

"You'll have to look at them," Andrea replied. "They're outside in the trunk of Leslie's car."

"I'll go out and get them." Jim headed for the door.

"Jim, I'm not sure you can carry all of them in one trip," Andrea said.

"All right, I'll get Hank to help me."

Andrea didn't say anything. She figured Hank would refuse.

A minute later, Hank came in to get his coat.

"That was nice of Hank," Leslie said, looking at Andrea.

"He probably didn't realize he'd be helping me."

She noticed a look pass between Jessica and Mary Jo. Then Mary Jo told them she'd hold dessert until the men were done.

"I'm not up for dessert tonight," Andrea said, eager to get out of the kitchen before Hank returned. "I think I'll go on to bed."

Jessica blocked Andrea's departure. "You at least need to show us what you bought this afternoon."

"Leslie can show you."

"If you think I'm going to demonstrate that cowboy outfit, you can think again, young lady," Leslie said with a laugh. "She put on quite a show in town."

Hank came in as Leslie was saying that. He halted abruptly. "What are you talking about?" His voice was harsh.

"Nothing bad, Hank. She was funny."

Andrea caught his scowl as he dumped the packages on the table and left out the back door.

"Come on, Andrea," Leslie invited. "Let's show them what we bought."

"No, I'm not feeling well. I need to get to bed." She rose and was on the stairs before Jessica could stop her.

"She was almost running up the stairs," Jessica said when she came back into the kitchen. "What were you talking about, Leslie? What did she do?"

"We were making up stupid situations where we would use the gifts. There was a sheriff's toy set, and she and the salesman did a hysterical skit. Nothing to cause her to hide."

"The last time she spoke to a man other than Hank, he was mad at her for days. Maybe she was afraid of Hank's reaction."

"Do you really think that's it?" Leslie asked.

"It's possible. Hank certainly looked mad."

DID HE HATE HER?

Andrea was stretched out on her bed, going over

what had just happened in the kitchen. Hank had looked so angry when he'd left. But why? Because of the horse or because she was fitting in with his family?

She knew only one thing for certain. She couldn't ride with him when he treated her as he had today.

But could she stay here? That was the real question she wrestled with. If he ignored her—

A soft rap on her door startled her. She got off the bed and approached the door. "Who is it?"

"Your dessert is here," said a muffled voice.

All right, so she knew Hank was outside her door. Should she open it? Her brain said no. Her heart said yes.

"Thank you, Hank," she said as she opened it.

Hank stood there with a plate in each hand. "How did you know it was me?"

"I recognized your voice. I've heard it enough."

"I told them you wouldn't open the door," Hank said, nodding over his shoulder.

"So do you want me to close it?"

He smiled that wonderful smile of his. "Only after you've invited me in."

When he looked like that, she couldn't resist. "Come in, Hank."

He moved past her. "Where shall I put these plates?" he asked.

She took one from him. "I only have one chair. As your hostess, I offer you the chair and I'll sit on the bed."

"I don't think we'll enjoy each other's company sitting so far away from each other."

After a pause, she said, "What do you suggest?"

"I think I should sit on the bed, too."

His offer was tempting, but Andrea had to be sure. "Hank, the last time we spoke, you weren't bringing me cake or speaking to me as if you even *liked* me."

He lowered his head for a moment, then looked up at her, his expression serious. "Honey, I made a mistake. Actually I made several. But the worst one was how I treated you. I didn't have faith in your ability. Will you forgive me?"

"It's not the first time you've misjudged me, Hank. I can only take so much."

"Won't you give a dumb cowboy a second—no, third chance?"

"Maybe, since you've been honest. But I think I want a little more information. Have you ever been involved in any long-term relationship?"

"Nope."

"Why not?"

"Because I hadn't met you."

"Come on, Hank. That's not—"

"It takes a while for me to warm up to people."

"Hank, that's not what—"

He leaned over and kissed her, silencing her.

For all her resolve to resist him, she had a hard time once his lips worked their magic on her. She felt herself giving in to his kiss, opening for him. But she couldn't let him just kiss his way out of trouble. She pushed him away.

"Andi, I was wrong," he said. "I know I made a mistake. But I want you to forgive me."

He reached for her again and she moved out of his grasp.

"Sweetheart, I've thought of a way to make up for what I said. I promised you an overnight trip. If we don't do it soon, we'll run out of time."

"Are you sure we can? I mean, Jessica can't go and—"

"We'll work it out."

Throwing her arms around his neck, she hugged him. "Hank, that would be wonderful!"

"Okay, I'll go downstairs and talk it over with the family."

She kissed him good night and closed her door behind him. Maybe she had misjudged him, after all.

"WELL, BOY, did she forgive you?"

Hank met his grandfather's gaze. "Yeah, she forgave me."

Cliff turned to Leslie. "I told you she would."

"But Granddad," Hank said. "I promised Andi I'd take her on an overnight camping trip."

"I told you how I feel about that, boy. You've got to have somebody else go with you."

Jessica was about to speak when Jim preempted her. "No way," he told her. "You are not going to risk our baby like that."

Pete spoke up. "Mary Jo and I can go. Jim can keep an eye on everything here."

Mary Jo sounded hesitant when she reminded him, "The season starts next week, Pete. I've got a lot to prepare."

"Aw, honey, I know, but I thought you could take a couple of days off so Hank could grant Andrea's wish."

Mary Jo sighed. "Maybe, but I can't let you know for sure until I sit down and see how much I have to do."

"Thanks, Mary Jo." Hank came over to hug his sister-in-law.

"I'm not promising anything yet, Hank."

ALL THROUGH BREAKFAST Andrea held her tongue. She didn't ask Hank anything about the trip until they were alone together on the way out to the barn.

"What did they decide?" she blurted out.

Hank hesitated and her spirits fell. "Well, Jess wanted to go because she remembered promising and she knows how much you want to go. But Jim said no, not with her being pregnant. Then Pete said he and Mary Jo would go…but he forgot to ask Mary Jo first."

"I guess the season starting so soon makes it hard," Andrea said, her voice full of resignation.

"Hey, I'm not giving up. I'm trying to work it out." He opened the barn for her and she went in. "Maybe we can still go."

Andrea's chin came up. "What do you mean?"

"I mean, I wouldn't take advantage of the fact that we were alone without any chaperones. I promise to behave myself."

"I think I'd appreciate your promise…and I accept the opportunity to go up the mountain."

"You do?" he asked, startled by her answer. "Really?"

"Really."

"When can we go?"

"Tomorrow morning?"

"That would be perfect."

"When we get back, I'll have to get some chores done, so I don't know if we'll have time to ride later."

"I can handle that." She walked to Moonbeam and stroked her neck. "This trip will be the perfect topper to my month."

Hank agreed. "I'll talk to Granddad at lunch. If he agrees, then we'll plan to go in the morning."

All morning as they rode they talked about the trip. Hank told her about the campsite they'd prepared and had used the past year. "Obviously we don't use it in the winter. So I'm glad to have a last chance to visit the place."

"Do you think we'll have good weather? I mean, there was a storm yesterday."

"Yeah, but not too much snow."

"What would happen if it snowed again?"

"If it got bad, we might have to stay a couple of nights."

"I think we'd better take warm sleeping bags."

"Don't worry, we will."

"Do I get to plan the food?"

"Sure. Though you might want to talk to Jessica."

"Afraid I'll schedule hot dogs for dinner?" she teased. "If I've learned anything about you, it's that you take your food seriously."

He gave her a sheepish grin. "I promise I'll eat anything you cook."

She knew better. "I'll talk to Jessica."

WHEN THEY RETURNED to the house for lunch, Hank washed up and set off for his grandfather's house, leaving Andrea alone with the women. She told Jessica and Mary Jo what Hank had promised.

Mary Jo gave her a pointed look. "Do you believe him?"

"Yes, I do," Andrea said.

"Are you sure?" Jessica asked. "I love my brothers, but I don't know about Hank's…appetite."

Appetite? Then she got Jessica's meaning. "Oh. I thought you were talking about his huge appetite for food."

"No, that's not what I'm talking about."

"I trust him, Jessica. He promised me."

After a long minute, Jessica nodded. "Okay."

"BUT GRANDDAD, I explained to her about the problems with Jess's pregnancy and Mary Jo's situation. She understood, but I couldn't refuse her. And she knew I meant my promise."

"That's nice, boy, but that don't mean much when there's no one else around."

"Andi trusts me. Why can't you?"

"Boy, I've seen the way you look at her. I'd like to believe you. But I have to be realistic."

"Granddad, I was hoping you'd come to trust me!"

Cliff shook his head. "Maybe Mary Jo will manage to make the trip."

"But she won't be able to get enough done. You know she's doing things in a rush as it is."

"Then you'll just have to plead with Jim to join you. That's your only hope."

"WHERE DID YOU GO?" Andrea asked Hank when she found him in the barn.

"To see Granddad."

"But you didn't come to lunch. Mary Jo fixed you a sandwich when you didn't show up. She didn't want you to go hungry."

"That's nice of her."

"I shouldn't give it to you, since you didn't even bother to come in." She gave it to him, anyway.

"I couldn't face them. I think you told them about my promise. While it would've felt good to hear you stand up for me, I was going to have to confess that my grandfather didn't believe me."

"You're kidding!" She frowned. "Your own grandfather doesn't trust you?"

"He said he's seen the way I look at you." Hank tossed the sandwich on a shelf.

"So he won't approve of us going up the mountain?"

"Not unless Jim goes with us."

Andrea sank onto a bale of hay. "I can't believe it."

"Honey, you may be the only one who believes in me."

"Then I think we should go, anyway."

Hank hesitated a moment, then took her hand. "Andi, I'm not sure *I* believe in my promise."

She understood what he meant. *Exactly* what he meant. "Then I *definitely* think we should go, anyway."

"But, Andi, I'm trying to tell you I don't know if I can keep my promise."

She stood up and wrapped her arms around his neck. "Hank, am I not making myself clear? I *want* you to make love to me on a mountaintop."

"Honey, I can't—"

"Yes, you can. My mind is made up."

"Don't you need to think about this for a while,

Andi?" He dropped a kiss on her forehead. "Honey, I want you badly, but this has to be mutual. Don't go just because you're mad about my family's behavior."

"I want it, too. I know how hard it is for you to go against your family, but that's what I'm asking. Will you take me up the mountain? Can we just leave on an overnighter without telling anyone? Just leave a note?"

He kissed her lips and murmured, "You bet."

Chapter Twelve

When they came in from riding, Hank went right to the barn to organize the equipment they would need for their overnight trip. Meanwhile, Andrea went to the kitchen and poured herself a cup of coffee. Fortunately, Mary Jo was there, as well as Jessica.

"You know, Hank and I were talking about the camping trip," she said slyly. "I don't really know anything about what we take for food."

Mary Jo said, "You can take almost anything."

"Will you do the cooking?" Jessica asked Andrea.

"I may be able to help out, but I don't know if I can handle everything. I've never cooked outdoors. Can Jim cook?"

"Jim? Why would you ask that?" Jessica asked.

"That's the only way your granddad will allow us to go on an overnight trip."

"But you said Hank promised to behave," Jessica said.

"He didn't believe Hank."

"Oh, poor Hank," Jessica said.

Andrea had more questions and they continued to discuss the camping details until Mary Jo finally said,

"Have you considered the fact that Jim might not be able to go? I mean, he has a lot to do before the start of the guest season, too."

"I know, Mary Jo. But I don't have much time left, either."

"We both know that. I wish you could stay longer," Jessica said.

"I know. But I have to go to… I have to leave."

"Maybe you'll come back again. Early summer is nice here." Mary Jo was stirring something in a bowl while she talked.

"What are you making, Mary Jo?" Andrea asked.

"Just a cake you can take with you when you go camping. It's nice to have something sweet." She shrugged. "If you don't go in a couple of days, I'll freeze it. Cakes always come in handy."

"What clothes do I need to take with me?" Andrea asked.

"Your long underwear!" Jessica replied. "Otherwise you'll freeze to death."

Andrea nodded, but she knew she had nothing to worry about. Hank would keep her warm.

ANDREA TOOK a shower and then dressed in a cotton shirt and jeans. Then she gathered what she would need for the trip in the morning—warm clothes and her long underwear.

They'd need sandwiches for lunch on the trail. Hank had said there was a fire pit at the campsite. He'd told Andrea that he could quickly build a fire when they arrived.

They had already discussed how they would get all the food they would take with them. Hank had told her they'd have to come to the kitchen after everyone had gone to bed. That worried her. They would have to be careful not to get caught.

Andrea went down to dinner with everyone, enjoying the camaraderie, something she appreciated more and more now that her time on the ranch was coming to an end. She hoped she could at least come back after she'd visited her father.

Would she be able to come back to Hank? How would she explain her decision to keep her identity a secret from him? She worried, too, how a rift between her and Hank would affect her future visits to her father; after all, the men were best friends. Her spirits sank as she thought about the future.

Then she straightened her shoulders. She had to be optimistic. She hoped *both* her dreams could come true—a relationship with her father and one with Hank.

It was after dinner that she made the decision to tell Hank the truth. They'd finally be alone tomorrow night with no chance of interruption. She'd tell him she was Dan Peters's daughter and explain why she'd kept it a secret. Surely Hank would understand. He had to.

As they watched television after dinner, Andrea kept looking at her watch. Time seemed to drag. Was no one in the household going to bed? She wanted to get on with their plan.

Finally, Jessica retired first, followed by Jim, and in no time everyone had gone to their rooms. Andrea sat on the edge of her bed for what seemed like hours as she waited for the clock to strike twelve.

At midnight she opened her bedroom door and stepped into the hall. She tiptoed past Jim and Jessica's room. It didn't seem anyone was still awake. When she reached the top of the stairs, she gasped and came to a complete halt.

At the foot of the stairs was a bobbing light.

She couldn't see the person, but something made her believe that it was Hank who carried the flashlight.

She started down the stairway, keeping her eyes fixed on the light and forming an alibi just in case. By the time she reached the bottom of the stairs, she could make out Hank's face.

"I thought we agreed on midnight," she said.

"We did, but I thought you'd be *there* at midnight." He shrugged. "That's all right, as long as you haven't changed your mind."

She smiled at him. "No, never."

"Good. Let's get busy."

In the darkness they scurried to the kitchen, where Hank immediately turned on the overhead light.

"Did you make a list?" he asked.

"Yes." She dug into her pocket and took out a piece of paper. Then each of them gathered the supplies they'd need. They certainly didn't want Mary Jo to figure out that they'd gone until evening. The next day they'd be on their way back home.

"I'll store everything in the cooler until we leave in the morning," Hank said.

"I'll put my things behind the stairs and pick them up on our way out."

"That should work. Give me a kiss, and I'll see you in the morning." He wrapped his arms around her as she leaned in and kissed his lips.

It was just a taste of the flavors to come.

ANDREA GROANED when the alarm woke her. She forced herself out of bed and padded into the bathroom. Then she remembered what made the day special. She and Hank were going into the mountains.

They'd spend the night there together. Just the two of them.

Hurrying through her morning routine, she ran down the stairs to breakfast.

Mary Jo had just served Hank his breakfast and he nonchalantly looked up from the flapjacks. "Morning," he said around a mouthful.

Hank was a much better actor than she was if his casual greeting was any indication. She could feel her heart beat faster and her cheeks heat just at the sight of him. And at the thought of what they'd soon be doing.

She busied herself at the coffeepot, got a grip on her nerves and finally took a seat in front of a plate of pancakes. Though she thought she could never swallow past the lump in her throat, she did.

Mary Jo had also made some of her famous apple-cinnamon muffins. Andrea was too full to try one and so she asked Mary Jo to pack up any extras that they could take with their lunch.

Andrea's insides twisted with guilt when Mary Jo happily wrapped up four of them. Little did she know they wouldn't be eating them during the day's lesson, but rather on their secret overnighter.

She was never so grateful when Hank told her it was time to saddle up.

With their extra muffins and their lunches, they set off for the barn, with only a brief stop behind the stairs for Andrea's stashed supplies.

When they were well out of earshot of anyone, Hank asked, "Did you write a note for the family?"

She reached into the pocket of her jeans. "Here it is."

Hank took it and read it. She'd told the family they'd tried to adhere to their wishes, but given the situation, they were going on the overnight trip without their blessing. No one should worry, as she was surely in good hands. Hank felt proud of that remark, but he wasn't so sure she should have spelled out to whomever read the letter what she hoped would happen.

"Is it okay?" she asked when Hank refolded the letter. "I didn't want to leave any unnecessary worries in their minds."

"It's fine," he told her. "Now go get Moonbeam out of the pasture."

"Want me to get your horse, too?"

"You don't have to. I'll get Jack after I load up the mule."

She took the bridle and walked out to the pasture. It didn't take long to capture Moonbeam; the mare had grown accustomed to her voice. Then she got Jack's bridle and moved toward Hank's favorite horse. She was surprised when he let her approach him. She managed to lead both horses over to the opposite side of the barn. Even though Hank's saddle was heavier than hers, she managed to saddle both horses, too.

When Hank started out of the barn for his horse, he stopped short when he saw Andrea with both of them bridled and saddled. "How did you manage that? Wasn't Jack's saddle too heavy?"

"It was a struggle, but Jack was very patient," she replied, pride in her voice.

"Then we're all ready to go."

"Did you get everything on the mule?"

"Yup, all of it. For two people and one night, we're taking an awful lot of stuff."

She looked around the pasture under cover of her hat. Seeing no one, she said, "Let's go while we still have a chance of sneaking away."

"I've got to lead Jenny, so leave room for her."

They mounted and then as they passed the far side of the barn, where they couldn't be seen, Hank quickly jumped down and got the mule. Setting off on their horses, they rode side by side, Hank holding the reins to the mule, who walked behind them with their supplies.

Andrea knew this was the trickiest part of the journey. Here they were visible to anyone who stepped out of the ranch house. She practically held her breath, sitting tightly in the saddle, her muscles bunched in preparation for someone calling their names.

Once they were on the trail, where they were less easy to spot, she let out a deep breath. In a short while, when they reached the north side of the mountain, they'd be home free.

"I don't think anyone saw us leave," she dared say to Hank.

"No, I think you're right."

They rode on, careful to keep a steady pace with Jenny trailing behind them. It was lunchtime when they made their first stop.

"Am I the only one starving to death?" Andrea asked him when they dismounted.

He shook his head. "I ate one of the muffins Mary Jo gave us, but that did nothing for me."

She laughed. "We're pretty pitiful, aren't we? All we think of is our stomachs." Not that that was true. She had other thoughts in her head—like what they'd be doing in a few hours when they made camp.

Andrea pulled off her gloves to get her lunch out of her saddlebag. "It's much colder than I expected."

"That's because the air is thinner up here."

"It must be really cold up on the mountain, then."

Hank mentioned the wind was picking up, too. "Do you think you can eat while you ride? I think it would be better for us to reach the campsite. It's sheltered there."

"Yes, I can manage." She patted her mare's neck. "Well, Moonbeam, you didn't get much rest. Can you take me again?"

If she wasn't mistaken, Moonbeam nodded her head.

"Did you see that? She answered me."

Hank laughed. "She's a good animal."

After she got into the saddle again, Andrea asked, "Who'll ride her next?" She hated to think there was a chance she'd never get to ride Moonbeam after this week.

"I don't know. It's hard to think about anyone else riding her."

"She's so gentle. I think she'd be good with any kids who visit the ranch."

"Probably." Just then there was a gust of wind, and Hank looked up at the sky. "We've got to get moving up that mountain. If I'm right, we're going to have snow soon. Looks like you're the snow maiden everyone's been waiting for."

Before they headed back onto the trail, he made sure she was prepared. "Is your coat zipped up? It's only going to get colder from here."

"Yes." Andrea reached up and settled her hat more firmly.

With a nod, Hank led the way onto the trail, pulling Jenny behind him.

An hour or so later Andrea felt the wind pick up. A blast of cold air hit them as they rounded the mountain, and she knew it was going to be difficult camping tonight. She ducked her head against the wind and hoped the campsite was as sheltered as he'd said.

Andrea was excited about camping out, but not in a snowstorm. Perhaps she should have come back in the spring and tried it then, but she couldn't think about leaving Hank without some resolution. She didn't want to let him forget her.

HANK WAS GETTING worried. His idea of making love to Andrea on top of the mountain wouldn't be quite as romantic as he'd hoped if they were freezing to death. He considered going back, but then Andi would be disappointed. He knew he could take care of her no matter what the weather, but huddling through a storm might not be as much fun as making love.

He turned to ask her a question. "Andi, you wore your long underwear, didn't you?"

"Of course I did. Otherwise I'd be a Popsicle by now."

"Good. I was just checking."

"Hank, is that what I think it is?" She looked up at the sky.

Snow had just begun to fall. "It is," he said with a sigh.

"Don't worry, Hank. We'll make it."

It was getting dark, but Hank was pressing on, hoping they could make it before sunset. He checked his watch. It would be dark by five, giving them only another half hour of daylight. He thought the campsite was a few minutes ahead, which would give them time to set up camp, or at least get a fire started before dark.

"Andi, are you doing all right?"

He heard a moan as he turned to check on her. He assumed that meant she'd be okay for a little while longer. "We should be there in just a couple of minutes."

Several inches of snow had already fallen. He guessed by now his family would have found Andi's note. He hoped they realized he'd take good care of her.

When he saw the next curve on the mountain trail, he knew he'd reached the right spot. He could see the fire pit and began envisioning flickering flames.

"We're here, Andi," he shouted back to her.

Hank knew she was too exhausted to be excited. He had to take care of the animals first, and the corral he and his brother had built for them was just around the corner. But first, he went and helped Andrea down.

"I'm going to build a fire just as soon as I take care of the animals." He found a rock for her to sit on and then grabbed the horses and headed for the corral.

When he was done, he removed Jenny's load and carried it to the fire pit. To his surprise, Andrea had been gathering firewood.

"Good job, Andi."

"I had to move to stay warm, anyway, so I thought I'd do something useful."

As soon as he coaxed a fire, he could put on more wood. He knew the warmth would make Andi happy. Him, too.

Once he had the fire going, he pulled out the tent. The sun had gone down, but in the glow of the firelight they could see enough to get it up. Andrea worked alongside him, despite his insistence that she stay near the fire.

She amazed him. A real trooper, she was nothing like the spoiled little rich girl he'd first thought her to be. She hadn't uttered one complaint the entire month, never complained about the work or aching muscles. And now, despite the cold and snow, she was silently working right beside him.

With the tent up, he pulled out the supplies for dinner. "Are you hungry?"

"Lunch seems like days ago. I think I could eat a bear if you had one."

"How about steaks?"

She smiled at him. "Sounds wonderful. I'll help you cook."

"No, I'll manage, but you could slice up the potatoes and then open the can of beans and put that on the fire."

"Are you going to put the steaks on the coals?"

"No, I'm going to let the fire burn for a while and then I'm going to put the steaks on a grill over the coals."

She got out the potatoes and beans. "If you want, I can make biscuits."

"You can? How'd you learn that?"

"Mary Jo taught me."

Though the snow was still coming down, they got busy fixing dinner. When they were finally able to eat, the food and the fire both made a difference.

"I FEEL MUCH BETTER now that I've eaten," Andrea said.

"Yeah. It's amazing what being outdoors will do for your appetite. You know steaks always taste better eaten outside."

She sent him a smile. "I wouldn't know, since this is my first experience eating outdoors."

"You're kidding! You haven't eaten outdoors?"

"No. Well, in New York, we eat on patios in front of restaurants, but I've never been to a cookout."

"We eat outside all the time, though I'll admit not when it's this cold."

"And not in a snowstorm?" she asked.

"No, not in a snowstorm."

Andrea stared into the fire. "Do you think the people who crossed the mountains to settle down and build a life out West only traveled on sunny days?"

He laughed at her. "No, Andi, I think they traveled every day. Except maybe in a wild storm."

"Will this storm be a bad one?" she asked.

Hank stared up at the night sky. "I don't think so. This is the beginning of the snowy months. Here, winter usually starts earlier than the first week of December. We've just been lucky so far this year. But I think this will spell the end of our warm fall."

"Will there be enough snow for skiers?"

"Yeah. By the time the snow stops, there'll be lots of fresh powder. Then you'll see the tourists come out in droves."

"I wonder if we'll be able to get back tomorrow."

"At least we'll give it a good try. The snow won't build up much on the trail. The wind will blow it away."

Despite being close to the fire, Andrea shivered. "I can't remember the last time I was warm." Actually it was this morning, under the covers of her bed. That felt like years ago.

"I put out the sleeping bags if you want to turn in."

She nodded, but he could see her in the firelight. "I want to warm up."

"Okay." He paused and then said, "I should tell you that I hooked our two bags together."

She expected nothing less. "I'll see you in a few minutes."

Hank gave Andrea fifteen minutes before he went to the tent. He thought that was enough time for her to get ready, but not long enough for her to fall asleep.

He gathered some firewood and covered it with a tarpaulin. It wasn't fun to try to build a fire made with wet wood, which caused a fire to smoke.

Once he'd done that, he checked on the animals one

last time, then finally made his way to the tent. His hand on the flap, he suddenly stopped. He debated what to do. Should he just go in or call out to her? He decided on the latter.

"Yes?" she replied when he said her name.

"I'm coming in." He opened the flap and ducked to enter.

"Is it still snowing?"

"Yeah, pretty heavily."

"Maybe it will stop in a little while."

"Maybe." He unzipped his coat, and when his eyes adjusted to the darkness he saw her eyes open wide. "Relax. It's just my coat. I don't have a zipper in my jeans."

Then he undid the buttons on his fly and shucked them in one quick motion.

Standing there in his thermal long johns, he looked down at her in her sleeping bag, so beautiful, so inviting. For a second he regretted that their first time together would be in these conditions. "Sorry I'm not coming right from a shower."

"I'm not worried. Now quit wasting time and get under the covers. I didn't think you were ever coming to bed."

He laughed. "I was afraid you'd think I was in too much of a rush."

"Get in here where it's warm."

He didn't waste any more words. He stepped out of his underwear and slid into the sleeping bag.

She gasped, and he immediately apologized.

"You didn't do anything. But your feet are ice-cold.

Maybe you should put your feet on my stomach. I've warmed up very nicely. Feel."

He put his hands on her stomach. "Very nice. I like it even better that you didn't put on a nightgown."

"I've heard it makes it easier to make love."

"Is that so? Did you learn that from experience?"

"Maybe." Then she volunteered her lips for a kiss.

HANK CARESSED her body, the gentleness of his touch shocking her. She'd seen those hands at work on the ranch, but now their calluses glided over her skin, leaving a trail of heat wherever they went. He seemed to be memorizing each curve and indentation of her body, the flare of her hips, the pinch of her waist. Finally, her breasts.

He deepened his kiss, their tongues mating, as he took her breasts in his hands.

She had waited so long for this moment, she could hardly believe it was happening. She wanted it to last forever, but Hank was such a masterly lover, he knew just what to do to set her on fire. She wanted him now.

That was when Andrea remembered what she'd forgotten. She stilled.

"Hank, I'm sorry, but I can't. I forgot…"

"What did you forget, sweetheart?" he asked, his voice husky, laced with passion. His hands continued to work their magic.

"I didn't bring any condoms with me."

He stopped then and looked down at her, his eyes dark and smoky. "Did you think that was your responsibility?" he asked softly.

"It usually is. Most men don't worry about protection."

"I've got protection. I'll take care of you."

Those words did more for her than his hands ever could. She captured his mouth in a fevered kiss that brought them both to the brink.

But she wanted to make this a night to remember, for Hank, as well.

She pulled her lips away from his mouth and began kissing her way down his chest, across his nipples. Her hands ran over every muscle in his abdomen and back, feeling his strength. She wanted to savor all of him. She wanted him to feel the passion she had brewing inside. Her hands dipped lower, down past his waist.

Hank stilled her touch. "Now it's my turn," he said, his voice hoarse. He turned her away from him and began kissing the nape of her neck and down her shoulders, all the while cupping her breasts in his hands, his thumbs grazing her nipples.

Andrea didn't think she could take much more and couldn't resist turning around to taste his lips again. He gladly accepted and pulled her tightly against him as their kisses deepened.

Both of them now breathless, Hank pulled out a condom and she enthusiastically helped him put it on. When he entered her, she thought nothing had ever felt so right. Their bodies seemed made for each other, moving in sync.

Hank was taking his time, looking down into her eyes as he set the pace. She gave herself over to him, body and soul, and let him see her emotions. She wanted him to know exactly what he was doing to her.

She called out his name and he drove into her more deeply, creating an amazing final climax for them both.

Then he offered her a sweet kiss. "That was wonderful."

"Mmm." She snuggled close, comfortable in his arms, not wanting him to ever move.

Finally he withdrew and settled down beside her. He held her tightly against him and she slept, totally satisfied.

Chapter Thirteen

Morning light streamed in, waking Hank. Eyes closed, he lay there, listening for the sounds of daybreak. Hearing nothing, he wondered if he'd woken up too early. Surely somebody would be moving around in the house. Certainly Andi would—

Andi! He'd almost forgotten the most wonderful night of his life!

Hank looked down to see Andi's face peacefully resting on his chest. It took only that one look to remember every detail of the night they'd spent together. She'd been everything he knew she'd be—confident, responsive, giving. Making love with Andi had been worth waiting for.

She looked so beautiful and content lying there, her hair splayed over his chest. He wished he could lie there longer, holding her in his arms, but he knew they had to hit the trail soon.

He checked his watch and realized they should have been up an hour ago. The trip home would be difficult and would take more time than it had coming out.

He gently kissed her. "Andi," he said against her lips.

"Mmm," she moaned, not quite awake.

Hank continued saying her name as he tried to pull them into a sitting position. At last Andrea's eyes opened, and as she looked at him, a smile crept across her face.

"Morning, beautiful," Hank said. "I hate to rush, but we enjoyed ourselves so much last night that we overslept. We need to get dressed, have some breakfast and get packed up as fast as we can. Okay?"

Most of her grogginess apparently gone now, Andrea said, "Okay, I can make breakfast as soon as I'm dressed while you pack up. Does that work?"

"That would be perfect." He gave her a quick kiss that turned heated. Knowing how quickly it could get out of control, he backed off. Standing up, he reached for his clothes and began to dress. "You know, we make a great team."

"Yes, we do," Andrea said as she lay in the sleeping bag waiting to get dressed until Hank had gone out to get the fire going again. The moment he had, she hurriedly pulled on her clothes. She longed for the warmth of the sleeping bag—and Hank—but they didn't have time to linger.

As soon as she was dressed, with her coat and hat on, she stepped outside the tent. Despite the still-falling snow, Hank had a nice fire going and must have gone around to the corral to tend to the animals.

She retrieved the skillet they'd packed with them, along with the bacon. In no time the heavenly smell of sizzling bacon filled the frigid air. She returned to the tent to pack the rest of her belongings in her bag. When she finished, the bacon was done and she began frying the eggs.

Hank had the tent rolled up just as she called him to breakfast. "It smells great, sweetheart," Hank said.

"How's Moonbeam this morning?"

"Perfect, just like her rider."

"That's sweet of you, even if it is a little overdone. Now eat your breakfast so we can go."

"Yes, ma'am," Hank said with a salute and a smile.

HANK HAD BEEN right. A lot of the snow had been blown away, but it was being replaced by fresh snow. Andrea hung on to her saddle horn, prepared for a slippery journey.

On one occasion Andrea thought she and Moonbeam were going over the edge, but the mare caught herself just in time. Andrea pulled to a stop, not quite able to continue for the moment. When she was ready to go on again, she urged Moonbeam forward.

Hank turned around. "You all right?"

"I am now, but I almost went over the side a moment ago."

"Sweetheart, you need to kick the stirrups free and jump toward the trail."

"I couldn't do that to Moonbeam! I'll be more careful."

"Ride in front of me. I'll yell if I think you have to jump."

"No, I like following your trail with the snow cleared a little. I'll just be more careful."

"Maybe I've been going too fast. I'll go slower."

After they started again, she slipped her feet out of the stirrups, which she really didn't want to do. She hoped she wouldn't have to abandon Moonbeam.

She thought about the sandwiches she'd made this morning. She'd cooked extra bacon and afterward had added sliced tomatoes. The food sounded so good to her right now, but breakfast had only been about two hours ago. She checked her watch to confirm, and sure enough it read almost ten o'clock. Just over two hours ago she was still asleep when Hank kissed her awake.

"What are you thinking about?"

She came back to reality to find Hank had stopped and had turned to stare at her.

"I was thinking about the way you woke me up this morning."

"Thank God. I was wondering who I was going to kill if you were thinking about someone else with that look on your face."

"Only you, Hank."

"Good. I'm going to hold you to that."

They rode on and she was so focused on the trail she didn't speak. Another hour passed slowly. But she couldn't stop her galloping thoughts. She couldn't stop thinking about how she was going to leave Hank.

Last night they'd been so busy with...other things that she hadn't told him everything she'd intended to tell him on this trip. Like the truth of who she was. Dan Peters's daughter.

Knowing this might be her only chance, she called his name.

"What is it, honey?" He twisted in his saddle.

"Do you remember what I said when I first arrived at the Lazy L?"

"The truth?" He grinned sheepishly. "I wasn't paying

attention to what you said then because I was so angry." He paused. "So did you want to tell me something?"

She wasn't certain how she could say it, where she should start. Probably it was best to just blurt it out and then backtrack. "I want to tell you I'm—"

"Hey!"

A deep masculine voice from somewhere ahead interrupted her confession.

Hank turned to face forward. She shifted her gaze from Hank and saw two riders coming toward them.

"Pete? Jim?" Hank said. "What are you two doing up here?"

"We were supposed to get up the mountain before… uh, well, we got delayed by the snow."

"Surely you didn't think you were going to get there before dark!"

"Granddad had us convinced we could get there in time."

"But Andrea and I left yesterday morning."

"We know," Jim said with a groan. "Mary Jo read us her note."

Hearing Mary Jo's name, Andrea remembered the cake that Mary Jo had made especially for their trip. "We forgot to take her cake."

"Yeah, Mary Jo was real disappointed in that," Pete said with a frown.

Hank defended them. "Come on, Pete, we appreciated Mary Jo's thoughtfulness, but we just had a lot to remember."

"And not much time," Andrea added.

"Speaking of not much time…" Hank looked around

at the still-swirling snow. "The snow hasn't stopped, so I suggest we get moving."

"Yeah, we don't want to stay up here any longer than necessary," Jim said. "I'm not happy spending so much time away from Jess." He was already turning his horse around. "Come on, Pete, let's get back to the ranch."

"All right, I'm coming, but you owe me, brother."

"It was worth the effort, Pete," Hank said with a big smile.

Andrea felt heat infuse her cheeks, despite the blustery wind and cold. Apparently the whole Ledbetter clan knew exactly what had happened between her and Hank up on that mountain.

"Andrea, come ride with me," Jim called out. "I promised Jess I'd keep you safe."

"I'll ride with Andi."

Hank's protests fell upon deaf ears and Andrea had to content herself with only memories of her tender cowboy.

WHEN THEY FINALLY got off the mountain trail, daylight had gone. Andrea was hungry and tired. They'd eaten the bacon and tomato sandwiches, but one sandwich had not been enough. She gave a wry smile. When she'd first arrived, she would have been satisfied. But now she was a cowgirl.

A cowgirl.

Her smile widened. It was true. Now she was ready to meet her father.

Hank came back to ride beside her as they crossed the pastures. They weren't alone and she couldn't talk to him the way she wanted to, but at least she had his company.

Once they got back to the Lazy L, the family would no doubt ask scores of questions, and she hated even to think what Cliff would say to Hank. Through it all, she probably wouldn't have another moment alone with Hank today. Certainly not another night.

But last night had been spectacular. The connection they'd shared had been unlike any she'd ever experienced with another man. Had Hank felt the same? She could only hope so.

"Do you see the lights, Andi?" Hank's voice broke into her thoughts. "We're almost home."

Yes. She'd seen the lights, and she was ready to be home—

The thought shocked her. Did she think of the Lazy L as home now? It did seem as if she'd been here forever, New York and her life there eons in her past.

They reached the stables all too quickly. Hank dismounted and came to Andrea's side. "I'll unsaddle Moonbeam for you, Andi. You go on up to the house."

"I can unsaddle my own horse, Hank."

"I know you can, sweetheart, but you're tired. Go ahead and let the women know we're starved."

"Okay. I'll tell them to hurry."

She slipped away, stifling the urge to kiss him for the last time today.

"ARE YOU ALL RIGHT?"

"Where's Hank?"

"Did the men find you?"

The questions hit her fast and furious. As soon as she'd entered the back door, Mary Jo and Jessica had wanted to know everything.

"One at a time," she told them. "We're fine. Hank's in the stable. And yes, Pete and Jim reached us on the mountain trail."

Mary Jo got her a cup of hot coffee to warm her up. "You guys had us worried. After I found your note and the snow started, we thought for sure you'd be stuck up there."

Andrea thanked her for the concern. "Hank took care of me. He was well prepared and he kept an eye on the weather. We had no trouble." Except for the slippery descent that almost killed her. But she didn't tell her new friends about that.

She looked around the kitchen. "Is Cliff here?"

"He's at his house, waiting out the storm," Jessica told her. "But he's not happy, I can tell you. He was very worried about you."

"And Hank, too, I'm sure."

"He knew Hank could take care of himself, but…"

"But I'm a greenhorn, right?"

"You're Hank's—and this ranch's—responsibility."

Andrea hadn't thought of it that way, but now she understood Mr. Ledbetter's concern. "I'm sorry," she said, shaking her head. "We didn't mean to cause any trouble. We just wanted to be…" She let her voice trail off.

Mary Jo gave Jessica a knowing look. "Alone. We know. It hasn't been that long since we were in your boots, you know."

Surprisingly Andrea wasn't embarrassed. There was nothing wrong with what she and Hank had shared last night. Nothing that felt that good could ever be wrong.

Right now, though, she wanted to keep it between herself and Hank. At least until she knew where their night of lovemaking would lead.

She had to talk to Hank alone.

WHEN WOULD HE GET Andi alone? All through dinner Hank had put up with the endless questions from his siblings and their spouses. Now that dessert was over, he wanted to steal Andi away for just a few minutes.

They needed to talk.

Last night had been amazing, but he needed to see where she thought this…relationship was going.

He'd had women before her, many women, in fact. But none had moved him the way Andi did. He dared to think he'd fallen in love with her. For a man like him, that was a scary realization, not to be taken lightly. He had no idea what it meant for them or where he went from here.

He only knew he wasn't about to tell her.

Not until he knew how she felt.

Given how Jessica and Mary Jo fussed over her like mother hens since they'd returned, he wasn't going to get the chance to ask her tonight.

The women had even ushered Andi up to bed. Jim had pronounced the hour late and en masse they'd gotten up from the sofas where they'd been nursing their coffees. While the men checked the animals one final time in the storm, Jessica and Mary Jo escorted Andi upstairs.

On his way up later, Hank had stopped in front of her door, but his brothers were right behind him and all he could do was utter a quick good-night.

Frustrated and confused, Hank lay on his bed, sleepless.

The only good thing, he realized, was that the snow had kept falling, keeping his grandfather away. He'd called the eldest Ledbetter when he'd returned, and judging from the tone of his voice, Cliff wasn't happy. What he had to say would best be said in person, he'd warned. So Hank had to wait until the weather cleared for his chewing-out.

He wished it would snow till spring.

Chapter Fourteen

Everything seemed back to normal the next morning. Jessica and Mary Jo chatted in the kitchen, the men had gotten an early start. The sky had cleared, but not before dropping close to a foot of snow. The Lazy L looked as if it'd been dipped in marshmallow topping, the horses and cattle dotting the landscape like chocolate sprinkles.

Andrea wasn't riding with Hank today—Jessica told her that he needed to organize the stable, and the snow prevented their riding out, anyway. So Andrea decided to do her laundry.

Later that morning, when the temperatures warmed up, she donned her boots and coat and hat and went out for a walk to enjoy the picture-postcard scenery. She strolled out to the pasture to check on Moonbeam.

When she passed the barn, she noticed Hank, and her heart leaped. He was working with Jim polishing up what looked to be the biggest sled she'd ever seen.

"What are you guys doing?" she called.

Hank looked up and a smile lit his face when he saw her. "Getting ready for sleigh rides. Now that we've got some snow, we can offer them to our guests. We've got our first batch arriving next week."

She waved to both men and continued on to the pasture with the apple she'd brought for Moonbeam.

The mare came up to Andrea and nuzzled her hand. Andrea fed her the apple, then put her arms around Moonbeam's neck and rested her cheek there. She'd come to love the mare. With her gentle disposition, she'd been a good horse for Andrea to learn on, and Andrea knew she'd miss her when she left.

Moonbeam…and Hank.

"WELL, BOY, you almost did it this time!"

Cliff Ledbetter's voice startled Hank as he concentrated on fixing the runner of the sleigh. Jim had called it a day and gone inside, but Hank was determined to get this contraption fixed. Keeping himself busy meant keeping his mind off Andi.

Now it seemed he had something else to occupy him. His grandfather.

Cliff stepped into the barn, the setting sun backlighting his imposing figure. His boot heels crunched the snow that had swirled into the barn as the men had worked.

"Granddad, let me explain."

His grandfather cut him off.

"Of all the stupid stunts you've pulled, this one is the winner. Do you know you could've destroyed everything we've worked for with this dude ranch? One slip on that trail and she gets hurt, she'd sue the Lazy L for everything it's worth. And then what would you do?"

"Andi wouldn't sue. She wanted to go."

Cliff waved off his reply. "Doesn't matter, boy. She's got family."

Could you really call her mother "family"? Didn't sound to him like the woman cared much about her daughter. Still, he took his grandfather's point.

"You were too busy listenin' to points south, weren't you. You didn't use your head."

Hank couldn't argue. He looked down, duly chastised.

"Now, we owe that woman an apology, and let's hope it's enough. I ain't worked my whole life for this ranch to leave it to my kin and have it go bust. So I expect you to behave yourself like a Ledbetter for the rest of her time here. You got me, boy?"

Hank nodded. "Yes, sir."

"Make that apology tonight." He turned to go back outside, and then stopped and pointed at the sleigh. "You gotta straighten out that runner."

Hank picked up the mallet and banged it hard, taking out all his frustration on the crooked runner. Damn. He just couldn't seem to do anything right.

First Jim and Pete and now his grandfather had reamed him out for his lack of judgment. Truth was, he deserved it.

And now he had to apologize to Andi. But not before he fixed the damn sleigh.

IT WAS AFTER TEN and Hank still hadn't come in. Andrea had waited for him, choosing to bypass the meal with the family so she could eat with him. But by seven-thirty she found herself eating alone in the kitchen.

Jim had said Hank was working on something important in the barn, something for Cliff, so Andrea hadn't dared disturb him. She didn't want to cause any more trouble between Cliff and Hank than she already imagined there was. She didn't know what was said between the two men this afternoon, but she'd heard their raised voices.

When the television program they were watching was over, Jim and Pete called it a night. Their wives assured them they'd be up shortly.

"You don't have to wait with me," Andrea told the women.

"Nonsense," Jessica said. "We'll sit awhile. We didn't have much of a chance to talk today, anyway."

Andrea sighed. "I'm not good company, I'm afraid. I'm too worried about Hank. Why hasn't he come in yet?"

"Don't worry, Andrea. My brother gets this way sometimes when he's got something to do." Jessica smiled. "It's a family trait. We're all a little stubborn."

Andrea didn't know how much of it was Hank's stubbornness and how much of it his desire to avoid her. No matter how often she told herself that the latter notion was ridiculous, she couldn't help coming back to it. After all, in the thirty hours they'd been back at the ranch, they'd said only a few words to each other. And those in the presence of Jim.

Mary Jo tried to distract her, talking about the delicious meals she'd planned for their first group of guests, and Jessica talked about the activities they'd organized. But Andrea hadn't heard much. At eleven o'clock, she gave up.

"I think I'll go up to bed," she said behind a yawn. "Thanks for staying up with me, but you guys need your sleep, too."

They walked upstairs together, leaving the kitchen light on for Hank. At Andrea's door, she turned to her companions. "Thanks again."

"Remember what I said," Jessica told her. "Don't worry about Hank."

Andrea knew she'd do nothing but.

IT WAS ALMOST midnight when Hank stepped into the kitchen, grateful for the plate of food he found in the fridge. He hadn't realized how hungry he was until he started eating the roast beef.

At least the damn sleigh runner was fixed, and the sleigh polished and ready to go. Heck, everything in that barn was fixed—all the tack, all the equipment. It was so spit-shined in there, it'd pass a full military inspection.

But while he'd been busy mending fences with his grandfather, he hadn't gotten to see Andrea all day. Nor had he been able to apologize to her.

The kitchen door creaked open then and he looked up from his dinner, hoping to see her. Jim walked in, instead.

"What are you doing up?" Hank asked him.

"Jess isn't feeling too well. She needs crackers to settle her stomach." He shuffled over to the pantry. "You get everything done out in the barn?"

Hank swallowed a mouthful. "Yeah. I hope Grand-dad appreciates it, at least."

"You know, Hank, you didn't need to do that. Cliff didn't mean for you to work yourself to death."

"I'm fine," he replied sharply.

Crackers in hand, Jim crossed to the table. "You know, what you really needed to do was talk to Andrea. She's not been herself since you came back."

Hank had worried about her all day. But right now he was sick of everybody telling him what to do.

He threw his fork down. "I make one mistake around here and you, Pete and Granddad are on me nonstop."

"Hank, we're only trying to help. We—"

"I don't need your help," he roared back. He didn't care about the hour, whom he woke up. He'd simply had it. "I don't need anybody. I was much happier when I was rushing out of here at night and heading into Steamboat Springs. I didn't have a care in the world then."

He pushed back his chair, grabbed his coat in a fist and stormed out the back door.

ANDREA COULD hardly believe her ears. She stood there at the door to the kitchen feeling as if a freight train had run over her. Her chest hurt and she couldn't seem to draw in a breath.

I was much happier when I was rushing out of here at night and heading into Steamboat Springs.

Had Hank really said that?

He had. And there was no denying it.

She'd come downstairs, eager to see Hank when she heard him come in. Now she wished she'd never laid eyes on him.

He'd taken her heart and stomped on it.

Tears stung her eyes and she let them fall. There was no one here to see her fall apart, so she let it happen.

She'd come down to tell him everything. Tell him about her father and how she was going to spend the holidays with him. Tell him that the more she thought about it, the more she didn't want to return to New York. She wanted to stay in Colorado. Tell him that she loved him and wanted a future with him.

Not now.

Now she had nothing to say to him.

She let out a small sob and leaned against the wall just as the kitchen door creaked open. Jim went past her, the crackers and a glass of water in his hands. He didn't see her.

Wiping her tears and taking a deep breath, Andrea waited a few minutes there in the darkness. Then she ascended the stairs, her mind made up.

She would leave the Lazy L in the morning.

Chapter Fifteen

Andrea waited in her room till the men rode out the next morning before she went downstairs. She found Jessica in the kitchen, talking with Mary Jo.

"Jess, are you busy?" she asked, trying hard to keep her voice nonchalant. She'd done all her crying last night. This morning she was determined to keep her emotions in check and do what had to be done.

"No," Jessica replied. "Did you need something?"

"I wondered if you could take me now."

Mary Jo stared at her. "Take you where?"

Jessica ignored her sister-in-law's question. Her face fell as she asked Andrea, "You're going now? But you still have a couple of days left."

"He's expecting me, and I'd like to go now. I've changed my sheets and cleaned my room, so it's ready for a new occupant."

"You didn't have to do that," Jessica said.

"It didn't take much time."

"Have you told Hank you're going?"

She'd been afraid Jessica would ask that. She kept to the script she'd mentally written last night. "No.

There's no time. He has a lot to do. Tell him goodbye for me."

"Wait a minute," Mary Jo said. "I still don't know where you're going."

Andrea took pity on the bewildered Mary Jo. She looked at her and said, "I'm going to Dan Peters's place."

"How do you know him?"

Andrea looked at Jessica, a question in her eyes.

"Yes, she can keep a secret."

"Dan Peters is my father. I haven't seen him since I was two."

Mary Jo gasped. "Does Hank know?"

Andrea shook her head.

"Why not?"

"I didn't tell him at first because I needed time to adjust, to prepare for meeting my father. Then I intended to tell Hank when we were up on the mountain, but…well, we were distracted."

"But won't he be angry that you left without talking to him?"

Andrea didn't answer. She simply asked Jessica, "Can you take me now? I've brought my luggage down and left it by the front door."

"Okay, I'll bring the car around. But first I get a hug."

Andrea hugged her and then Mary Jo. Despite her resolve to avoid any difficult emotions, she had to lower her head to hide her tears.

When Jessica pulled the car up, Andrea loaded her luggage and they drove the five miles to her father's house.

"You're sure he's expecting you?"

"Yes." Tears were running down her face now.

Jessica reached over and took her hand. "I know how you feel about Hank. Andrea, please tell me what happened."

"I—I can't."

"What will I tell him?"

She hated putting Jessica in this position, but she had no choice. "Tell him it was fun while it lasted." She wiped her tears. "Promise me this time you won't tell anyone where I've gone. I don't want anything to ruin my visit with my father."

"I promise, Andrea." She gave her a hug. "We're going to miss you a lot."

"Me, too."

She'd never been more sincere.

ANDREA GATHERED herself to walk up the drive to her father's house and ring the doorbell. Her heart beat a rapid tattoo in her chest and her palms were damp as she waited.

The door was opened by an attractive blonde. "Yes?" the woman said. She sounded irritated.

Andrea cleared her throat. "I—I'd like to see Dan Peters."

"He's busy right now. Can I help you?"

"Is the housekeeper busy?"

"I'll see," she said coolly, and walked down the hall.

Andrea was so nervous that if she had a car, she would've driven away. She was about to *run* away when two little boys came to the door.

"Who are you?" the older of the two asked.

"I'm here to see Dan Peters."

"He's our daddy."

"He's my daddy, too."

"Really?" the younger boy asked, his eyes wide.

"Really."

The little boy turned and ran to his mother, who was coming back up the hall. She ignored her son's words and said, "The housekeeper can't come to the door right now. I'm afraid I'm the only one available. Frankly, I'm not interested in magazines or whatever else you have to sell."

"I don't have anything to sell. Dan invited me to come for Christmas."

The woman's eyes widened. "Are you Andrea?"

She nodded, suddenly unable to speak.

Smiling now, the woman invited her in. "I'm so sorry, I thought you were selling something. Charlie, go tell your daddy to come here at once."

"If he's busy…" Andrea began to say.

"Oh, no, he's waiting for you to arrive. I finally sent him to the barn because he was getting on my nerves. Did you meet my sons?"

"Sort of. Charlie and Casey, right?"

The woman offered a warm smile. "Yes, and I'm Barbara. Now you know all of us." She held out a hand, which Andrea shook.

"I'm delighted to meet you, Barbara."

They moved into the living room. "Please sit down and forgive my lack of hospitality," Barbara said. "Chalk it up to insanity due to my pregnancy."

Andrea laughed and sat in a comfortable chair

opposite her father's wife. "I heard you're having another boy."

"You did? Who told you?"

"I took riding lessons at the Lazy L, and Jessica mentioned that you were having a boy."

"Jessica's so nice."

"Yes, she is. Her baby will be born not too long after yours."

"I didn't know she was expecting. Did you hear that, Dan?" Barbara said to the man who'd just entered the room.

Andrea jumped to her feet and stared at her father. The father she hadn't seen since she was two.

She'd gotten a glimpse of him at the ranch a couple of weeks ago, but this was the first time she'd seen him face-to-face. He was handsome, clearly an outdoorsman, with blue eyes. Exactly the way she'd always pictured him.

He walked up to her. "You've grown up since I last saw you."

"I'm afraid so," she managed to say through a suddenly dry throat.

"Can I have a hug?"

For months since she'd made her decision to meet him, she'd wondered what his reaction to her would be. Only in her wildest dreams had she heard him ask for a hug.

She rushed into his embrace, almost sobbing.

"I was afraid you wouldn't really come." His voice, too, sounded husky and rough.

"I actually came a month early to take riding lessons."

"Riding lessons? Where did you… Hank? You're Hank's pupil?"

She nodded and lowered her head. "I know you probably think it's stupid, but I just had to learn to ride before I met you. I wanted you to be—" She stopped herself before she could say it.

"Proud of you?" her father filled in. He didn't wait for her reply. "You didn't have to learn to ride to make me proud of you. I already am."

She looked up. "You are?"

"Yes, and I've been counting the days to your arrival."

It sounded so good to hear him say that. "I asked Mother about you a number of times. She never gave me an answer."

"What did she tell you?"

"She told me you didn't want a child."

Her father ran a hand through his hair. "That woman couldn't be trusted then and she can't be trusted now."

"It's okay if you were too young to be a father."

"Honey, I wanted you from the first moment I saw you. But she kept me away. She used her family's money to ensure she got custody and to take you as far from me as possible."

"I didn't know."

He reached for her hands. "Well, she can't keep me away now."

No, Andrea thought. Now that she'd found her father, nothing would keep her away.

"HAS HANK COME IN yet?" Jessica asked Mary Jo as she walked in the door after taking Andrea to her father's.

"No, no one has."

"When they do get back, let's not mention Andrea's departure."

Mary Jo held up her hands. "I know nothing. I saw nothing. But she got there all right?"

"Yes, she wanted me gone before she rang the doorbell. I thought I should make sure they would take her in, but I know Dan. He's too nice to leave her on the doorstep."

They both heard the back door slam.

"I think that's Hank," Jessica said.

They stood and watched the door.

Hank came into the kitchen, his eyes searching the room. "I'm going upstairs to find Andi."

Jessica and Mary Jo looked at each other.

"I'd better go break the news to him." Jessica sighed as she followed Hank up the stairs.

When she reached the bedroom Andrea had occupied, she found Hank staring into it, his expression stunned.

"What happened?" he asked. "She was here earlier."

"Don't you remember what she said when she first came to the Lazy L?"

He shook his head.

"She said she was visiting someone after her lessons ended."

"Immediately? Without even saying goodbye? How close was she to this person?"

"I don't know. She just said she had to go."

Hank still stared into the room, as if not believing Andrea wasn't there. "But I thought after that night on the mountain… I thought she cared…"

Jessica's heart broke for her brother. But she'd made a promise to a friend and she had to keep it.

"I don't know, Hank."

He stood there, saying nothing.

"I've got to go help Mary Jo," Jess said at last. "Why don't you get cleaned up for dinner?" Then she turned and ran down the stairs.

ANDREA WAS GONE.

Hank still refused to believe it. He went into the room and looked in the closet, opened every drawer in the dresser. All were empty.

How did she leave the ranch without him knowing?

And why had she left?

Admittedly they hadn't seen much of each other since they got back from their overnighter, but surely Andrea hadn't been angry about that. She knew how he felt about his grandfather and how important the ranch was to him. Would she hold it against him that he'd worked hard to win back his grandfather's approval?

No, not Andrea. Not the Andrea he was in love with.

Could he have been wrong about her?

He remembered their night together, how she'd responded to his kiss, his touch. How she'd sighed beneath him. How she'd made him feel like he was the most important man on earth.

Unless she was one hell of an actress, she cared for him as much as he cared for her.

So why did she leave? And why didn't she tell him?

The questions were still on his mind when he went down to dinner.

He noticed that Mary Jo and Pete and Jim seemed unusually quiet when he entered the kitchen. No one wanted to make eye contact with him. Did they know something?

"Where's Jess?" he asked when he saw only four place settings at the table.

"She went into town to pick up some more Christmas decorations," Jim answered.

"By herself?" He thought that was strange. Ever since she'd announced her pregnancy, Jim had been so protective of her.

Jim seemed to hesitate before he replied, "You know your sister when she's got something on her mind." He took his seat. "Shall we eat?"

Throughout dinner they talked about everything but Andrea—the snow, the new horses, the upcoming season, the guests who would be arriving soon. Finally Hank couldn't take it anymore. He put down his knife and fork and simply blurted it out. "Isn't anyone going to ask me why Andrea left?"

Total silence descended on the room.

After a few moments Pete spoke. "All right. I'll ask you, just like I've been asking my wife."

Hank shook his head. "I don't have a damn clue why."

"I thought things had been going great between you two," Pete said, "especially after your night on the mountain."

"So did I."

Something made him look up at Mary Jo then. He thought he detected a slight flush to her cheeks. Unlike her husband, she kept her eyes down, as if concentrating on her food.

"You don't know anything, do you, Mary Jo?"

She looked up and met his eyes. "No. Sorry, Hank."

Whatever hope he had died with that response. He pushed back his chair and got up from the table. His appetite was gone.

Chapter Sixteen

Should she...or shouldn't she?

Like a magnet, the phone drew Andrea's eyes to it. No matter how often she tried to turn her gaze away, it kept coming back.

She knew the only way she could move on with her life was to make a clean break. Yet more than anything she wanted to call him, talk to him, tell him where she was and who she was.

But what good would that do? she asked herself. Hank had made it clear what he'd wanted from her. And it was not happily ever after.

She argued with herself for hours, seeing the sun come up and then hearing the household start to rouse. Finally she threw off the bedcovers, resigned to the fact that she'd gone another night without sleep.

Forcing herself to look on the bright side, she turned her thoughts to her father. He was, after all, the reason she'd come out West and started this whole insane journey. She may have lost the man she loved, but she'd found the father she never had.

A smile on her face, she dressed and went down to share breakfast with her stepbrothers.

Charlie and Casey chattered nonstop, asking her all kinds of questions and talking about how their lives had changed since their mother married their daddy.

"Do you mind if we call him Daddy?" the older boy, Charlie, asked around a mouthful of Froot Loops.

Andrea shook her head. "Not at all. I can see that you love him and that he loves you, too."

Charlie said, "Yeah, he tells us that all the time."

"You're very lucky."

"Daddy is going to teach us to ski!" Casey said. He was sporting an adorable milk mustache.

"That's great. Your mother, too?"

"No, she can't ski. She's too fat!" Casey shouted.

Andrea laughed. "Your mommy isn't fat, Casey. She's going to have a baby, and that's what happens."

"Why?" the boy asked.

"That's a question your daddy should answer for you."

"All right. Let's go ask him." Charlie abandoned his cereal and started for the barn, dragging his little brother with him.

Andrea followed them out to the barn where her father had his office.

"Let's race!" Charlie said, knowing he was already in the lead. Though she ran pretty fast, Andrea wasn't about to race and leave Casey behind, his little legs pumping hard to eat up the distance between him and his brother. Instead, she kept pace with the younger boy and made it to the barn just ahead of him.

"I almost beat you!"

"Yes, you did…almost."

Inside the barn, she could hear Charlie excitedly calling out to their father. She stepped into the office with her stepbrothers and smiled at their father. "Sorry to bother you, but we needed to consult with you this morning. I hope you have time for us."

Dan turned away from his computer and gave the three of them his full attention. "What do you need to talk about?"

"Well, the boys don't seem to understand why their mother is gaining weight. Casey thinks his mom is getting fat. When I tried to explain that she's pregnant, they didn't understand. I thought maybe you could explain what'll happen in April, and how they'll need to be patient."

Dan nodded, looking somewhat uncomfortable. "I told Barb we had to have this talk. I guess now is the time." He looked at the boys as if unsure where to even begin.

"Well, you see…" He met Andrea's gaze and smiled uneasily.

She gave him a quick hug and a pat on the back. "You know what? I think I'll leave you to your man talk."

Her father shook his finger at her. "I'll get you for this."

Andrea just laughed as she walked out of his office.

Amazingly, in just a day, she and her father had gotten to a place where they could joke with each other. It felt good. The man had been an enigma to her all her life, but the moment she met him she felt as if she'd known him forever. He was warm and caring, open and honest.

Exactly the opposite of her mother.

She realized then that she couldn't go back to New York. Funny thing, she'd stopped thinking of New York as home ever since she'd fallen in love with Colorado. The Lazy L and her dad's ranch felt more like places she belonged.

But how could she stay out here when she couldn't be with Hank?

ANDREA WAS THRILLED when her dad asked her to go riding several days later. Showing off her newly acquired skills, she dazzled him on a long ride around his ranch.

When they drew their horses up from a gallop to a trot, Dan praised her. "Hank did an amazing job teaching you. How much did you ride in New York City?"

"I'd never been on a horse in my life until I was introduced to Moonbeam. She's wonderful, by the way."

"I'm glad you liked her. She's a fine animal."

"Why did you sell her?"

"Because she was a mistake. The sire was sold to me as a true Appaloosa, but when she was born, I knew he wasn't what I'd bought. I gave the sire back and the seller returned the purchase price. Moonbeam was a special filly, but she wasn't a purebred. Since I only deal with purebreds, I sold her to Hank."

"Well, I'm glad you did."

They continued to trot around the ranch, Andrea enjoying her time with her father and the brisk sunny day. "How did your talk with the boys go, by the way?"

Her dad laughed. "They had some interesting questions that they're going to surprise their mother with."

"Poor Barb!"

"Speaking of Barb, she asked me when you were going home."

Andrea went so tense she nearly pulled up her mount. "Have I worn out my welcome already?"

"Oh, no! I didn't mean to give you that impression. In fact, Barbara thinks you should stay here, even after the holidays are over."

Andrea let out the breath she'd been holding, her heartbeat going back to normal. "I'm glad. I like it here."

"What are your plans?"

She shook her head. "I don't really have any. But I do know I don't want to go back to New York."

"You don't?" He pulled up his horse and looked at her, a huge grin on his handsome face.

She couldn't help but smile back. "I'm a cowgirl now, Dad."

"Those words are music to my ears." If she wasn't mistaken, he sounded as if he was going to cry.

Tears stung her eyes, too. "Maybe there's more of you in me than Mom thought."

He reached over and hugged her as best he could with them both on horseback. Andrea knew she'd made the right decision. Right here was where she wanted to be. With her father.

"You know you're welcome to live with me, honey," he said as they walked their horses toward the barn. "Or if you'd prefer to be more where the action is—" he waggled his brows "—there's a lot of places in Steamboat Springs. Nice condos with young people like yourself."

Andrea shrugged. "I don't know, Dad. It's all so new. I mean, I've just made my decision. I think I need time."

"If you don't mind my asking…isn't there someone special back in New York?" He walked his horse into the barn and dismounted. "A pretty girl like you must have a guy. I imagine you've left a broken heart or two along your way."

Broken heart? Andrea thought. *She* was the one with the broken heart. Hank had stolen it, then smashed it to pieces, unlike any man she'd ever been involved with. Finding another man was the last thing on her mind right now. She just wanted to give herself some time to heal.

She dismounted, then finally answered, "No, Dad. There's no one."

He seemed surprised. "No one at all?"

What was it about this man that he could see right through her, despite not having laid eyes on her in more than twenty years? Or had Hank told him something?

"Have you been speaking to someone at the Lazy L?" she asked tentatively.

"No. Why?"

His innocent reaction assured her that no one at the Lazy L had been indiscreet. But in the end, she had no choice but to tell the truth.

At least part of it.

"There was someone I was in—" She stopped herself, changing it to "Someone I met."

"At the Lazy L?" From the look in his eye, she could tell his mind was working, no doubt going through the roster of men at the neighboring ranch. "Who? Jim and Pete are married, and Hank…" He laughed again. "Let's just say he's one heck of a confirmed bachelor. One of the hands?"

Her heart sank and she hung her head, trying to hide behind her horse as she began unsaddling him.

"Andrea?" Her father made his way around her Appaloosa and looked directly at her. "Is there something you want to tell me?"

With nowhere else to hide, Andrea met his eyes. "It's Hank."

Apparently that was the last name her father expected to hear. She had to hand it to him, though; he caught himself before he could overreact. "Hank," he repeated. So much was conveyed in that one little word.

"I know, Dad. He's not the man for me."

"He's a great guy, honey, and a good friend. But he's not the marrying kind." Her dad took off his hat and ran a hand through his thick hair. "If I know you, you want marriage and a family, but I'm afraid he can't give that to you."

Tears fell down her cheeks and she went into her father's outstretched arms. Through her sobs she whispered, "I know."

HANK HUNG UP the phone and turned back to Pete and Jim, who'd just come in from tending to their first group of guests. He'd called Andi's home back in New York and spoken to the housekeeper. The woman's English wasn't the best, but she had managed to convey the simple truth: she had no idea where Andrea was. The only number she had was the one at the Lazy L.

Pulling out a kitchen chair, Hank dropped into it, feeling more dejected than frustrated. He had nowhere else to turn. He'd already spent a few nights in Steamboat Springs, going from one restaurant and hotel to another, hoping to catch a glimpse of her. If she didn't go there, then where? As much as he would like to, he couldn't search the entire state of Colorado. Assuming she'd even stayed in the state.

The time had come to face facts. Andi was gone for good.

"I'm sorry, Hank."

He looked up at Jim. "I can't believe it. I really thought we had something special." Hank had always prided himself on his knowledge of women. This time, though, he'd been clueless.

"I know how it feels, bro," Pete said. He'd gone through a similar trial with Mary Jo, but lucky for him, they'd worked it out.

"Did you talk to her about what would happen after her month was finished?" Jim asked.

"No, I thought I'd have time to persuade her to stay here. But she didn't give me a chance." He thought for a moment. "Maybe I'll go to New York and camp outside her door. She's got to go home sometime, right?"

"Hank, don't be crazy."

"Wouldn't you go no matter what distance to find Jessie?"

"Well, yeah."

"I feel the same way about Andi."

Jim nodded. "Why don't you wait until tonight after dinner, and we'll all put our heads together."

Hank agreed.

Jim clapped him on the back as he checked his watch. "It's time for dinner. Let's go mingle with our guests."

But food held no appeal for Hank. Neither did the trio of single young women who were among their guests.

"I CAN'T TAKE THIS anymore, Mary Jo. We've got to do something." Jessica had pulled her sister-in-law aside in the hallway after their husbands had gone to bed. It had been after twelve by the time the last guest had retired for the night and they'd held their family powwow on behalf of Hank.

"He's got it bad. You saw him tonight. He's lost weight. He doesn't talk to any of the guests. This afternoon Jim told me he forgot his riding lessons. The guy's a mess."

"You're preaching to the converted, Jess," Mary Jo replied.

"But Andrea begged me not to tell him."

"And Hank's your brother." She let the words sink in, then added, "Whose side are you on?"

Jessica needed no further argument. "I've got to do something."

"Are you going to tell Hank where she is?"

"No. I've got another idea."

THE WEEK at the dude ranch had gone incredibly smoothly. During the day the guests went skiing at the Steamboat Springs ski resort, where they got reduced lift tickets and rentals. The Steamboat Springs Ski Counsel sent the Lazy L referrals, and the ranch was fully booked for the next three weeks.

But for Jess the best part of the week was tonight's big Christmas bash, with sleigh rides and Santa Claus making an appearance for the kids.

Pete was going to be Santa and Hank was driving the sleigh. All the guests would be there for their final night on the ranch—including some very special visitors.

Jessica had invited the Peters family.

Her phone call to Dan was a thing of beauty, if she said so herself. She'd told him it was the holiday season kickoff and he was to bring the whole family.

"The whole family?" Dan had asked, a slight lilt to his voice.

"Yes. We specifically want the whole family."

"I see. Then I accept."

Technically speaking, Jess hadn't divulged anything Andrea made her promise not to tell. But she'd get Andrea to the ranch—with Dan's help.

When Hank came down for the party, he questioned the extra table in the dining room, and Jess told him that Dan and his family would be joining them.

Mary Jo put out a special holiday buffet of such beauty it resembled a magazine cover. The singing cowboys, who'd been such a hit on Wednesday night, came back for an encore and were warming up their Christmas songs. And Jess put out the gifts she'd wrapped for the children.

When the guests convened in the dining room for punch and hors d'oeuvres, Jim sidled up to her.

"I'm impressed, Jess. You've done a marvelous job. Now if we could only get Hank to smile."

She kissed his cheek. "He will tonight."

The doorbell rang and with two trays of sausage rolls in her hands, she called out for Hank to answer it.

She thrust the trays into her husband's hands and tiptoed behind Hank to the door. She couldn't wait to see his face when he opened it.

"DAN, HI. I'M GLAD you could come."

Hank shook Dan's hand and greeted his wife and their two sons. He took the bottle of wine that Barbara offered him and then moved to shut the door on the blustery wind. Dan's voice stopped him.

"I hope you don't mind, Hank, but I took the liberty of bringing my daughter."

"Your daughter?" Hank's brows drew together. "I didn't know you had a daughter."

"Then allow me to introduce her." He pulled open the door all the way. "Andrea Jacobs."

Hank lost his grip on the bottle of cabernet.

Dan's quick reflexes saved it.

Hank stood there, speechless.

"I wanted to tell you," Andrea said softly, her eyes barely making contact with his, "but it just never seemed to be the right time."

He shook his head. "Forgive me, but I'm lost."

"Dan's the father I hadn't seen practically my whole life. I came out here to learn to ride so I could impress him when I finally met him. It was his house I was going to after the ranch, to spend Christmas with him."

Her words sank in, but Hank could hardly believe that after the suffering he'd endured the past week, Andi was standing in front of him. "You mean you've been at Dan's place the whole time and I didn't know?"

"Yes."

He smiled at the irony of it all. He'd been planning to go two thousand miles and she was fifteen miles away.

But there was still a gap between them that had to be bridged. He'd be damned if he'd do it in front of an audience.

"Andi," he said, "I need to talk to you. But not here. Would you mind going somewhere private?"

She looked away and his hopes fell.

But then she simply said, "Yes."

He led her to the barn, which was the only place he was sure they'd have privacy. The night air was cold, but he was willing to withstand anything to settle whatever had happened between them.

She walked immediately to Moonbeam's stall. "Hey, girl," she cooed to the mare who recognized her immediately and nickered. She patted her neck. "I missed you."

"I missed you, too, Andi," Hank whispered to her.

She looked at him, her lips tight and her eyes hard to read. "Did you, Hank?"

"How can you ask that? You know how I felt about you."

She nodded her head and turned away. "Yes, I do. I overheard it, clear as day."

Hank had no idea what she was talking about. Overheard what? Chills crept up his arms and legs that had nothing to do with the cold.

"I overheard you talking to Jim the night before I left."

He still didn't follow. "What did I say?" What could he have said to make her leave him?

She faced him then and her eyes that had seemed so emotionless before now were angry. "I heard you tell Jim how you were better off when you were hanging out with your women in Steamboat Springs." Her eyes glittered and she raised her head. "Apparently I was too much trouble for you."

Hank's breath gushed out of him as if he'd been hit by a charging bull. He remembered that night. He'd argued with Jim because everyone had been on his case. His grandfather had just finished chewing him out and then Jim had started in on him. He'd said things…no, he'd shouted things that he didn't mean.

And Andi had heard them.

He moved toward her, but she backed up against Moonbeam's stall. "Andi, let me explain."

"What's to explain, Hank? I know the kind of guy you are. You were honest from the beginning. You have no intention of settling down with a wife and kids. You told me all that. I guess I just didn't listen till that last night."

"No, it's not like that." He ran a hand through his hair. "I said those things to Jim that night because I was frustrated. My grandfather lashed out at me that afternoon and I didn't want to listen to Jim's lecture, too. I just didn't know what to do. I had to please my grandfather and that meant I couldn't see you."

"Hank, please," she said as she put up a hand. "You don't have to do this. I came here tonight to get closure. That's all."

He felt as if his heart had been ripped out. "No, Andi. I don't want closure. I love you." There, he'd said it. Those words that he thought he'd never say.

"It doesn't matter what you say, I—" She stopped abruptly, her hand shaking now, her brow knitted. "What did you say?"

"I said I love you."

Tears flooded her eyes as she looked at him, and a tiny sob escaped her lips. "I…I love you, too, Hank."

He'd begun to think he'd never hear those words from her. Before she could say anything else, he ran to her and took her lips. He wrapped his arms around her and pulled her close—exactly where she was meant to be.

He let her go only long enough to smile into her eyes, then he kissed her again.

She giggled then and Hank pulled back.

"It's Moonbeam," she said. "She's nuzzling my neck."

He laughed. "She's happy you're home. And so am I."

She gave him a brilliant smile. "Yes, I am home." She stood on tiptoe and kissed him.

"So you're through with your women?" she asked him as she held his face in her hands.

"Every one of them but you." Amazingly that was true. Andi was the only woman he wanted to be with. "Can you stay the night? I don't want to let you leave this ranch ever again."

She smiled up at him. "I don't know, Hank. You'll have to ask my father."

"How 'bout I ask your father if I can marry you, instead?"

Tears glistened once again in her eyes and she placed a kiss on his lips. "To that, I'd say yes."

Epilogue

Andrea looked at herself in the mirror and could hardly believe that today was her wedding day. She was marrying Hank Ledbetter.

She'd packed her bags and moved for the last time, taking her things from her father's house to the Lazy L. This was where she intended to spend the rest of her life, with Hank, with his family, and with her family only a few miles away.

She'd be living with the man she loved and next door to her father, in time to see his fourth child born, her own little brother. And maybe one day, she'd have children, too. As a matter of fact, she anticipated Hank would want children before too long. Pete was already campaigning for his own child to grow up with Jessica and Jim's.

Not that she objected to children. But after all this turmoil, she looked forward to having Hank to herself for a while.

Now that she'd left her job in New York and was unemployed, she figured they'd be spending days and nights together. Hank had asked her to help with the horses and riding lessons when the dude ranch was open for business. In the off-season, she figured she could do some freelance graphic design. The Lazy L was her first client, Cliff having hired her to redesign their logo and brochure.

Her life couldn't get any better than this.

Downstairs she could hear Mary Jo and Jessica putting the finishing touches on the banquet table and decorations. Andrea had insisted they have the wedding at the Lazy L, since that was where their romance had begun. Hank insisted they marry right away, since he couldn't wait long to make love to her again. It was all the Ledbetter wives could do to get him to wait a week so they could make the day one to remember.

Andrea checked her reflection once more, declared her gown ready, put on her lipstick and opened the door. Her father was waiting for her in the hall.

"Are you ready?" he asked.

She took a deep breath and let it out slowly. "Yes."

"Then let's go get you married." He held out his arm to her and she wrapped her hand around it.

They walked to the top of the stairs; below she heard the strains of the wedding march, but in a Western style, courtesy of the cowboys. Her father held her back before she could take the first step.

"Before you go, I want to tell you something." He swallowed hard and turned to face her. "You know, I never thought I'd get to have you in my life and here I am walking you down the aisle." His eyes filled with tears. "I'm the luckiest man on earth." Then he shook his head and said, "No, Hank's the luckiest man on earth."

Andrea kissed her father's cheek. "I love you, Dad."

Arm in arm, they descended the steps and then walked slowly up the makeshift aisle, formed by rows of chairs in the emptied-out living room. In its corner, the giant Christmas tree sparkled with miniature white lights, and she remembered the day they'd all decorated it. In front of her, the fireplace was lit with dozens of red and green candles, giving her wedding the holiday glow she'd always dreamed of.

Andrea's smile bloomed brighter as she noticed the people who'd come to share this day. Barbara was holding Casey in her arms, with a fidgeting Charlie at her side. Cliff had his arm around Leslie, who was already crying tears of joy. On the other side of the aisle, Mary Jo beamed from ear to ear as she held Pete's hand, and Jessica and Jim gave her a thumbs-up.

And to her great surprise, in the front row was the one person she'd never expected to see. Her mother. She nodded and smiled as Andrea walked by. They had some talking to do later.

She kissed her father and stepped up to the makeshift altar in front of the fireplace. There stood Hank, in a black suit and bolo tie, looking handsome and strong and sure.

He met her eyes and smiled, and Andrea knew he'd always be there for her.

When the minister pronounced them husband and wife, Andrea realized she'd gotten the best present ever. A cowboy for Christmas.

* * * * *

Here is a sneak preview of
A STONE CREEK CHRISTMAS,
the latest in Linda Lael Miller's acclaimed
MᴄKETTRICK *series.*

A lonely horse brought vet Olivia O'Ballivan to Tanner Quinn's farm, but it's the rancher's love that might cause her to stay.

A STONE CREEK CHRISTMAS
Available December 2008
from Silhouette Special Edition

Tanner heard the rig roll in around sunset. Smiling, he wandered to the window. Watched as Olivia O'Ballivan climbed out of her Suburban, flung one defiant glance toward the house and started for the barn, the golden retriever trotting along behind her.

Taking his coat and hat down from the peg next to the back door, he put them on and went outside. He was used to being alone, even liked it, but keeping company with Doc O'Ballivan, bristly though she sometimes was, would provide a welcome diversion.

He gave her time to reach the horse Butterpie's stall, then walked into the barn.

The golden retriever came to greet him, all wagging tail and melting brown eyes, and he bent to stroke her soft, sturdy back. "Hey, there, dog," he said.

Sure enough, Olivia was in the stall, brushing Butterpie down and talking to her in a soft, soothing voice that touched something private inside Tanner and made him want to turn on one heel and beat it back to the house.

He'd be damned if he'd do it, though.

This was *his* ranch, *his* barn. Well-intentioned as she was, *Olivia* was the trespasser here, not him.

"She's still very upset," Olivia told him, without turning to look at him or slowing down with the brush.

Shiloh, always an easy horse to get along with, stood contentedly in his own stall, munching away on the feed Tanner had given him earlier. Butterpie, he noted, hadn't touched her supper as far as he could tell.

"Do you know anything at all about horses, Mr. Quinn?" Olivia asked.

He leaned against the stall door, the way he had the day before, and grinned. He'd practically been raised on horseback; he and Tessa had grown up on their grandmother's farm in the Texas hill country, after their folks divorced and went their separate ways, both of them too busy to bother with a couple of kids. "A few things," he said. "And I mean to call you Olivia, so you might as well return the favor and address me by my first name."

He watched as she took that in, dealt with it, decided on an approach. He'd have to wait and see what that turned out to be, but he didn't mind. It was a pleasure just watching Olivia O'Ballivan grooming a horse.

"All right, *Tanner,*" she said. "This barn is a disgrace. When are you going to have the roof fixed? If it snows again, the hay will get wet and probably mold..."

He chuckled, shifted a little. He'd have a crew out

there the following Monday morning to replace the roof and shore up the walls—he'd made the arrangements over a week before—but he felt no particular compunction to explain that. He was enjoying her ire too much; it made her color rise and her hair fly when she turned her head, and the faster breathing made her perfect breasts go up and down in an enticing rhythm. "What makes you so sure I'm a greenhorn?" he asked mildly, still leaning on the gate.

At last she looked straight at him, but she didn't move from Butterpie's side. "Your hat, your boots—that fancy red truck you drive. I'll bet it's customized."

Tanner grinned. Adjusted his hat. "Are you telling me real cowboys don't drive red trucks?"

"There are lots of trucks around here," she said. "Some of them are red, and some of them are new. And *all* of them are splattered with mud or manure or both."

"Maybe I ought to put in a car wash, then," he teased. "Sounds like there's a market for one. Might be a good investment."

She softened, though not significantly, and spared him a cautious half smile, full of questions she probably wouldn't ask. "There's a good car wash in Indian Rock," she informed him. "People go there. It's only forty miles."

"Oh," he said with just a hint of mockery. "*Only* forty miles. Well, then. Guess I'd better dirty up my truck if I want to be taken seriously in these here parts. Scuff up my boots a bit, too, and maybe stomp on my hat a couple of times."

Her cheeks went a fetching shade of pink. "You are

twisting what I said," she told him, brushing Butterpie again, her touch gentle but sure. "I meant…"

Tanner envied that little horse. Wished he had a furry hide, so he'd need brushing, too.

"You *meant* that I'm not a real cowboy," he said. "And you could be right. I've spent a lot of time on construction sites over the last few years, or in meetings where a hat and boots wouldn't be appropriate. Instead of digging out my old gear, once I decided to take this job, I just bought new."

"I bet you don't even *have* any old gear," she challenged, but she was smiling, albeit cautiously, as though she might withdraw into a disapproving frown at any second.

He took off his hat, extended it to her. "Here," he teased. "Rub that around in the muck until it suits you."

She laughed, and the sound—well, it caused a powerful and wholly unexpected shift inside him. Scared the hell out of him and, paradoxically, made him yearn to hear it again.

* * * * *

*Discover how this rugged rancher's wanderlust
is tamed in time for a merry Christmas, in
A STONE CREEK CHRISTMAS.
In stores December 2008.*

Silhouette®

SPECIAL EDITION™

FROM *NEW YORK TIMES* BESTSELLING AUTHOR

LINDA LAEL MILLER

A STONE CREEK CHRISTMAS

Veterinarian Olivia O'Ballivan finds the animals
in Stone Creek playing Cupid between her and
Tanner Quinn. Even Tanner's daughter, Sophie,
is eager to play matchmaker. With everyone
conspiring against them and the holiday season
fast approaching, Tanner and Olivia may just get
everything they want for Christmas after all!

*Available December 2008
wherever books are sold.*

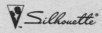

SPECIAL EDITION™

MISTLETOE AND MIRACLES

by *USA TODAY* bestselling author

MARIE FERRARELLA

Child psychologist Trent Marlowe couldn't believe his eyes when Laurel Greer, the woman he'd loved and lost, came to him for help. Now a widow, with a troubled boy who wouldn't speak, Laurel needed a miracle from Trent…and a brief detour under the mistletoe wouldn't hurt, either.

Available in December wherever books are sold.

HARLEQUIN® Romance®

Marry-Me Christmas

by *USA TODAY* bestselling author

SHIRLEY JUMP

A *Bride* FOR ALL *Seasons*

Ruthless and successful journalist Flynn never mixes business with pleasure. But when he's sent to write a scathing review of Samantha's bakery, her beauty and innocence catches him off guard. Has this small-town girl unlocked the city slicker's heart?

Available December 2008.

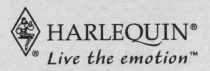

HARLEQUIN®
Live the emotion™

REQUEST YOUR FREE BOOKS!

2 FREE NOVELS PLUS 2
FREE GIFTS!

Love, Home & Happiness!

YES! Please send me 2 FREE Harlequin® American Romance® novels and my 2 FREE gifts (gifts are worth about $10). After receiving them, if I don't wish to receive any more books, I can return the shipping statement marked "cancel." If I don't cancel, I will receive 4 brand-new novels every month and be billed just $4.24 per book in the U.S. or $4.99 per book in Canada. That's a savings of close to 15% off the cover price! It's quite a bargain! Shipping and handling is just 25¢ per book, along with any applicable taxes.* I understand that accepting the 2 free books and gifts places me under no obligation to buy anything. I can always return a shipment and cancel at any time. Even if I never buy another book from Harlequin, the two free books and gifts are mine to keep forever.

154 HDN EEZK   354 HDN EEZV

Name	(PLEASE PRINT)

Address		Apt. #

City	State/Prov.	Zip/Postal Code

Signature (if under 18, a parent or guardian must sign)

Mail to the Harlequin Reader Service:
IN U.S.A.: P.O. Box 1867, Buffalo, NY 14240-1867
IN CANADA: P.O. Box 609, Fort Erie, Ontario L2A 5X3

Not valid to current subscribers of Harlequin® American Romance® books.

Want to try two free books from another line?
Call 1-800-873-8635 or visit www.morefreebooks.com.

* Terms and prices subject to change without notice. N.Y. residents add applicable sales tax. Canadian residents will be charged applicable provincial taxes and GST. Offer not valid in Quebec. This offer is limited to one order per household. All orders subject to approval. Credit or debit balances in a customer's account(s) may be offset by any other outstanding balance owed by or to the customer. Please allow 4 to 6 weeks for delivery. Offer available while quantities last.

Your Privacy: Harlequin is committed to protecting your privacy. Our Privacy Policy is available online at www.eHarlequin.com or upon request from the Reader Service. From time to time we make our lists of customers available to reputable third parties who may have a product or service of interest to you. If you would prefer we not share your name and address, please check here. ☐

HAR08R2

Harlequin® Historical
Historical Romantic Adventure!

THE MISTLETOE WAGER

Christine Merrill

Harry Pennyngton, Earl of Anneslea,
is surprised when his estranged wife,
Helena, arrives home for Christmas.
Especially when she's intent on
divorce! A festive house party
is in full swing when the guests
are snowed in, and Harry and
Helena find they are together
under the mistletoe....

*Available December 2008
wherever books are sold.*

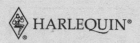

HARLEQUIN®

American ★ Romance®

COMING NEXT MONTH

#1237 A BABY IN THE BUNKHOUSE by Cathy Gillen Thacker
Made in Texas
When Rafferty Evans offers the very pregnant Jacey Lambert shelter from a powerful rainstorm, the Texas rancher doesn't expect to deliver her baby! Now, with five cowpokes ooh-ing and ahh-ing over the new mom's infant, can Jacey help the handsome widower open his heart to the love—and instant family—she's offering?

#1238 ONCE UPON A CHRISTMAS by Holly Jacobs
American Dads
Is Daniel McLean the father of Michelle Hamilton's nephew? As Daniel spends time with the young Brandon, and helps Michelle organize Erie Elementary's big Christmas Fair, the three of them come to realize a paternity test won't make them a family. But the love Michelle and Daniel discover just might…

#1239 A TEXAN RETURNS by Victoria Chancellor
Brody's Crossing
Wyatt McCall just blew back into town, still gorgeous, still pulling outrageous stunts like the ones he did in high school. And the stunt he's planning this time around could reunite him with the woman he loves. Mayor Toni Casale, who still hasn't gotten over Wyatt, has no idea what the Texas bad boy has in store for Brody's Crossing—and for *her*—this Christmas!

#1240 THE PREGNANCY SURPRISE by Kara Lennox
Second Sons
Sara Kauffman is lively, spontaneous, playful—everything Reece Remington is not. Although he's only visiting the coastal Texas town where she lives, Reece has a surprisingly good time helping Sara run a local B&B. Could this buttoned-down guy be ready for an entirely different kind of surprise?

www.eHarlequin.com

HARCNMBPA1108